SCARY GRAPHICS

ROAD TRIP TERROR

STONE ARCH BOOKS
a capstone imprint

Published by Stone Arch Books, an imprint of Capstone
1710 Roe Crest Drive
North Mankato, Minnesota 56003
capstonepub.com

Library of Congress Cataloging-in-Publication Data
Names: Foxe, Steve, author. | Brown, Alan (Illustrator), illustrator.
Title: Road trip terror / by Steve Foxe ; illustrated by Alan Brown.
Other titles: Scary graphics.
Description: North Mankato, Minnesota : Stone Arch Books, an imprint of
Capstone, 2022. | Series: Scary graphics | Audience:
Ages 8–11. | Audience: Grades 4–6. | Summary: Louis is totally bored by
the family's road trip with his younger sister, and the tacky tourist places
they stop at, but when his sister climbs out the window of the motel at the
worn-down Prehistoric Action Park he goes out to search, and suddenly the
dinosaur statues seem a lot more scary—and strangely mobile.
Identifiers: LCCN 2021008478 (print) | LCCN 2021008479 (ebook) |
ISBN 9781663911766 (hardcover) | ISBN 9781663911773 (pdf) | ISBN
9781663911797 (kindle edition)
Subjects: LCSH: Amusement parks—Juvenile fiction. | Dinosaurs—Juvenile
fiction. | Brothers and sisters—Juvenile fiction. | Graphic novels. | Horror
tales. | CYAC: Graphic novels. | Horror stories. | Amusement parks—Fiction.
| Dinosaurs—Fiction. | Brothers and sisters—Fiction. | LCGFT: Graphic
novels. | Horror fiction.
Classification: LCC PZ7.7.F69 Ro 2021 (print) | LCC PZ7.7.F69 (ebook) |
DDC 741.5/973—dc23
LC record available at https://lccn.loc.gov/2021008478
LC ebook record available at https://lccn.loc.gov/2021008479

Editor: Abby Huff
Designer: Heidi Thompson
Production Specialist: Tori Abraham

Printed and bound in the USA. 004270

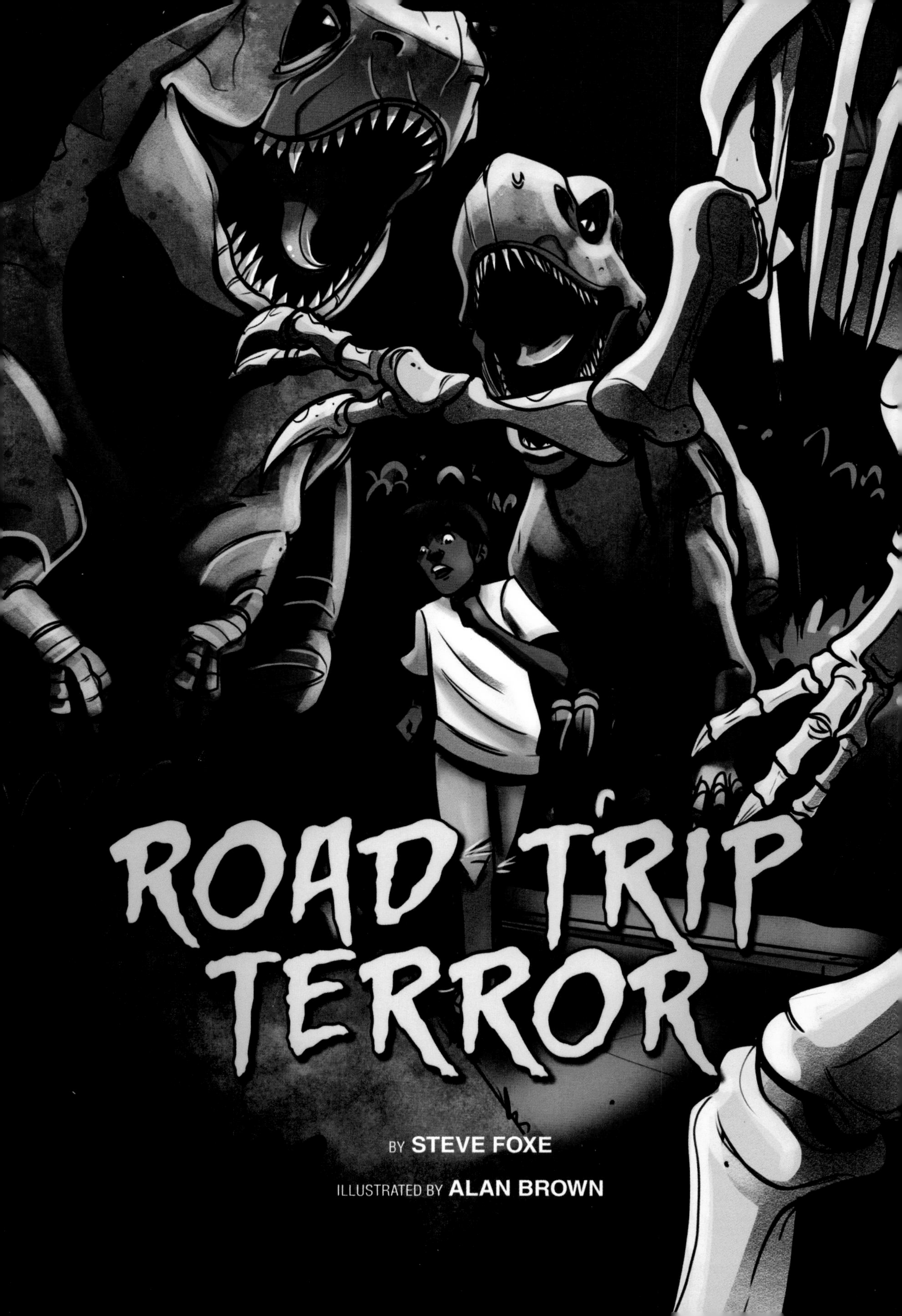

ROAD TRIP TERROR

BY **STEVE FOXE**

ILLUSTRATED BY **ALAN BROWN**

WORD OF WARNING:

SOME TERRORS NEVER GO EXTINCT.

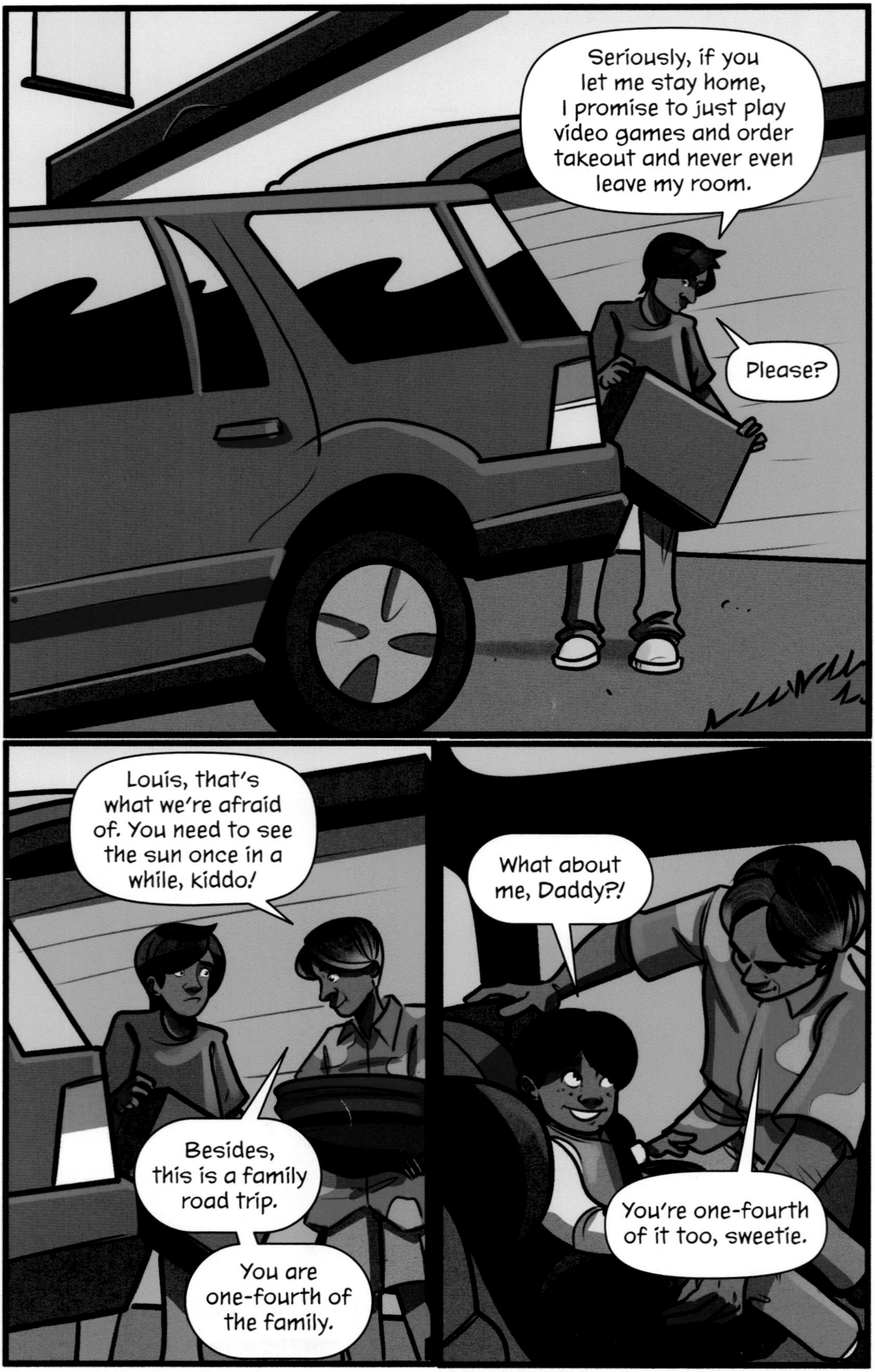
Seriously, if you let me stay home, I promise to just play video games and order takeout and never even leave my room.
Please?
Louis, that's what we're afraid of. You need to see the sun once in a while, kiddo!
Besides, this is a family road trip.
You are one-fourth of the family.
What about me, Daddy?!
You're one-fourth of it too, sweetie.

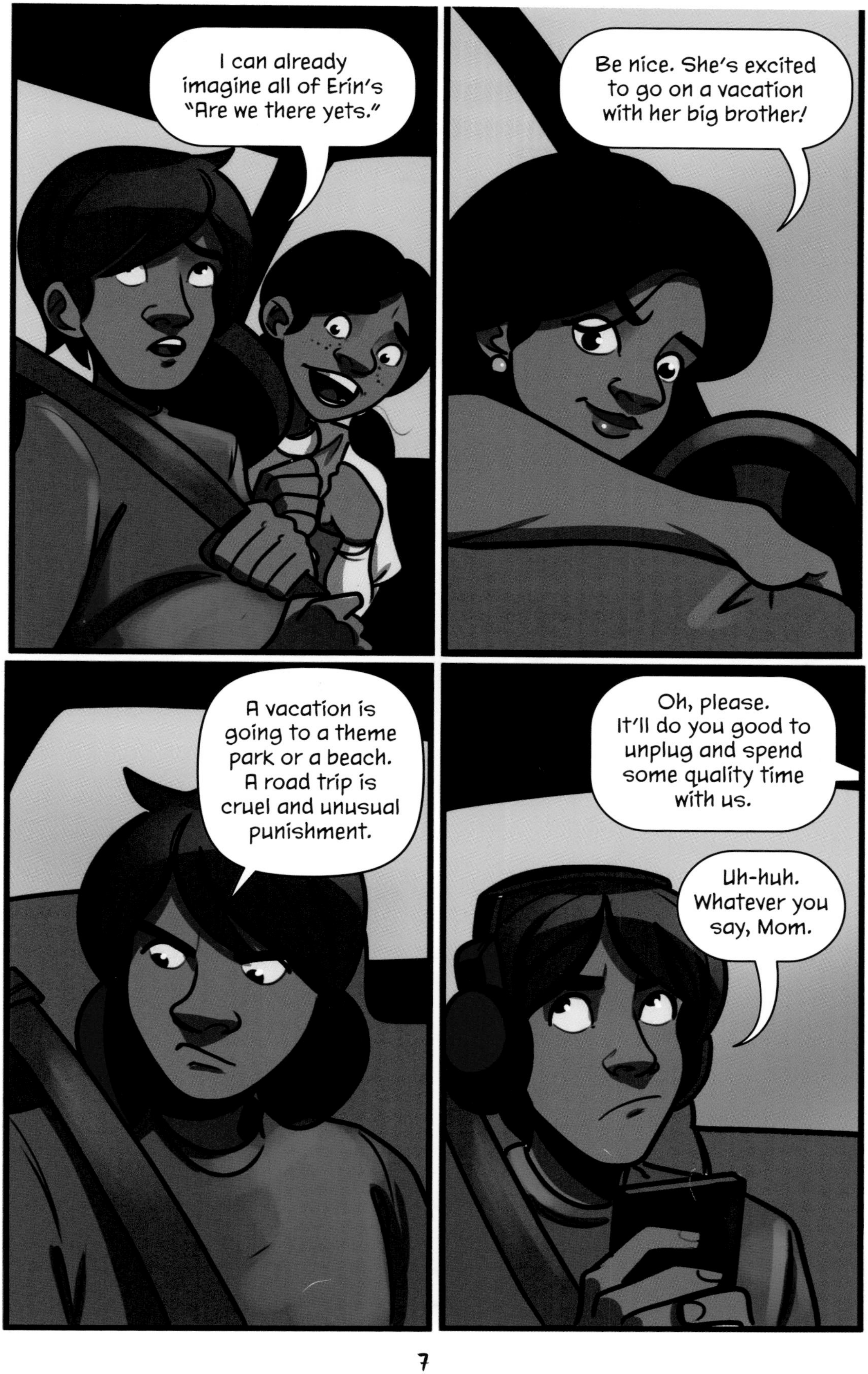
I can already imagine all of Erin's "Are we there yets."
Be nice. She's excited to go on a vacation with her big brother!
A vacation is going to a theme park or a beach. A road trip is cruel and unusual punishment.
Oh, please. It'll do you good to unplug and spend some quality time with us.
Uh-huh. Whatever you say, Mom.

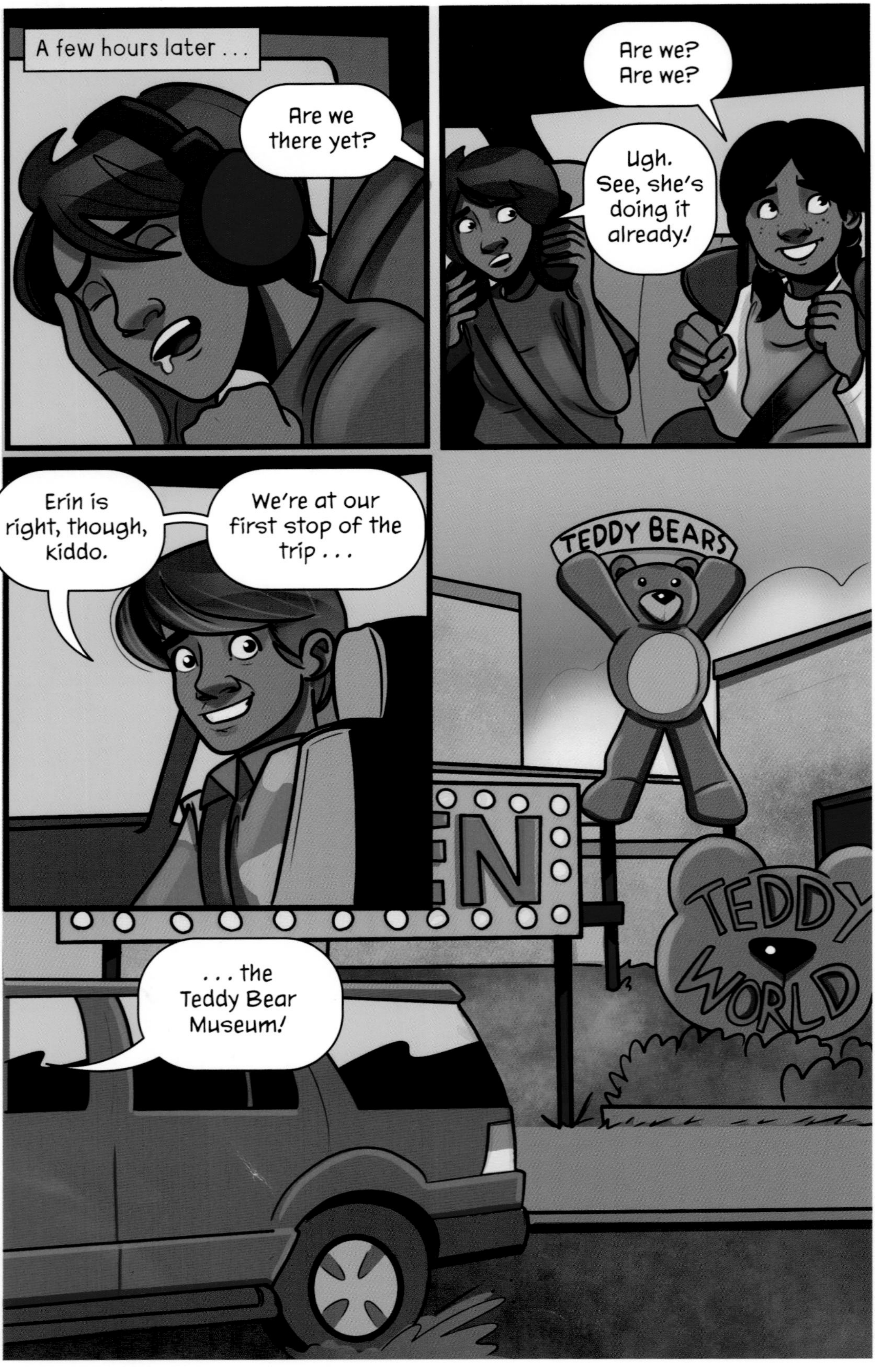
A few hours later . . .
Are we there yet?
Are we? Are we?
Ugh. See, she's doing it already!
Erin is right, though, kiddo.
We're at our first stop of the trip . . .
TEDDY BEARS
EN
TEDDY WORLD
. . . the Teddy Bear Museum!

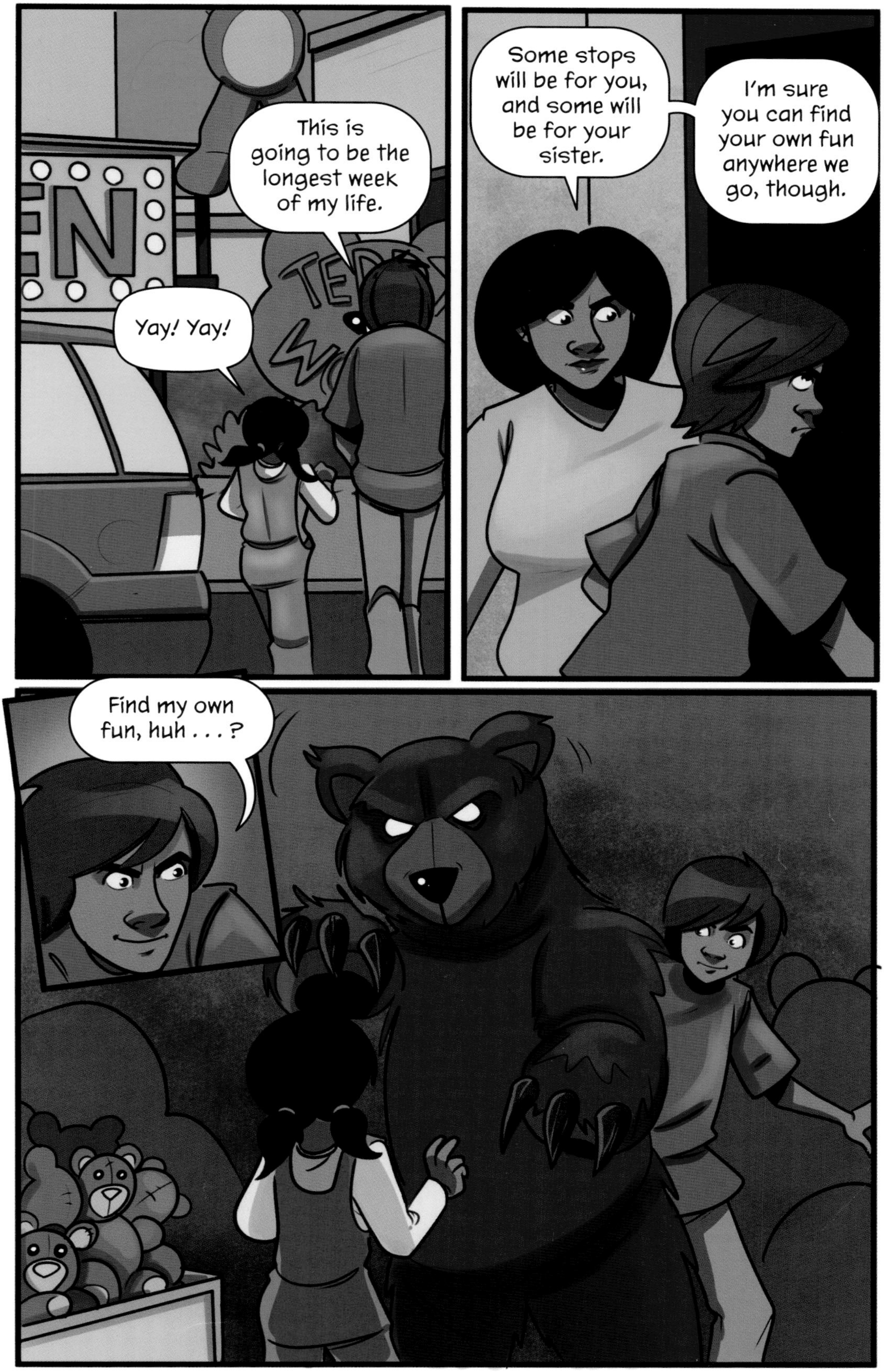
This is going to be the longest week of my life.
Yay! Yay!
Some stops will be for you, and some will be for your sister.
I'm sure you can find your own fun anywhere we go, though.
Find my own fun, huh . . . ?

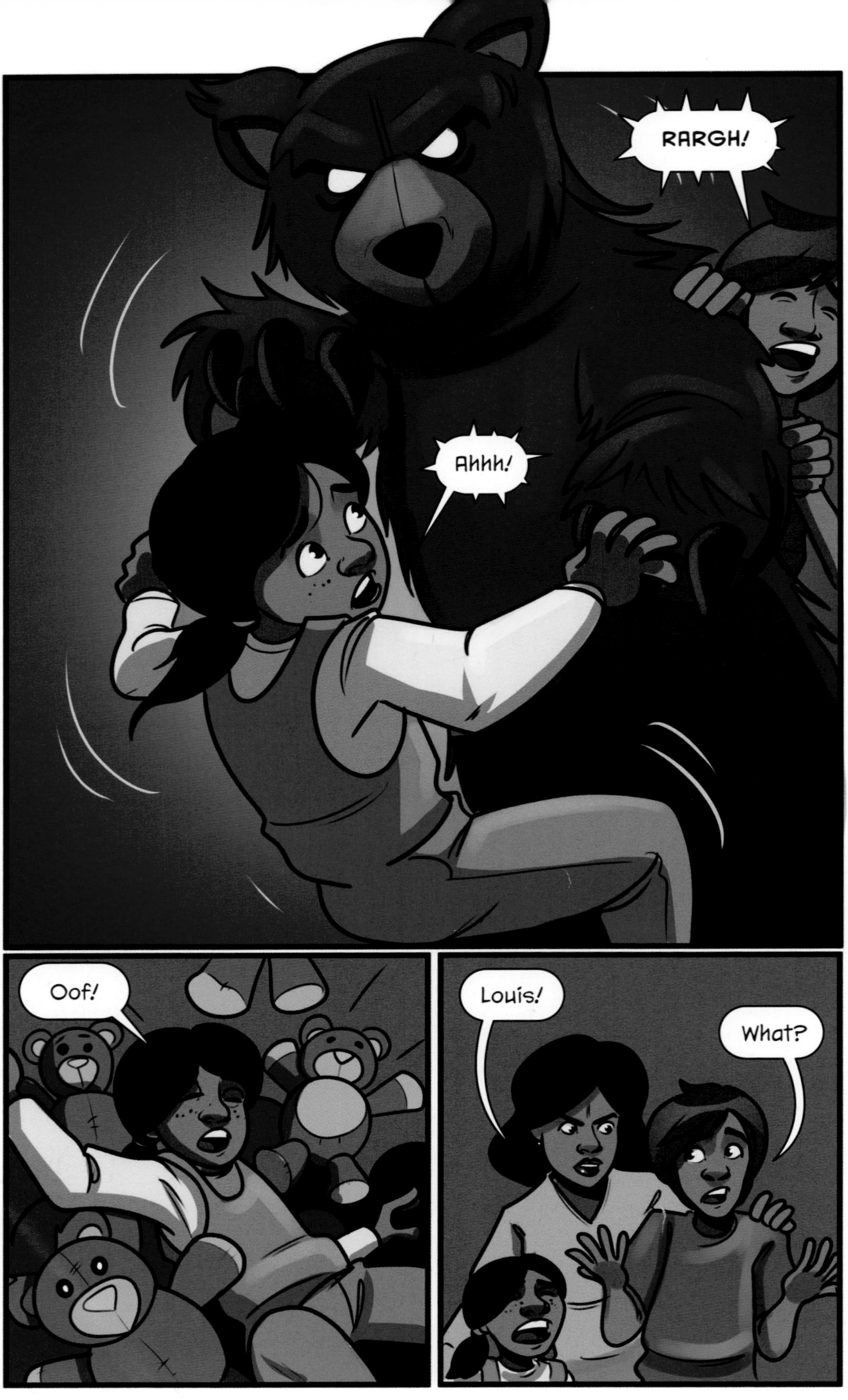
RARGH!
Ahhh!
Oof!
Louis!
What?

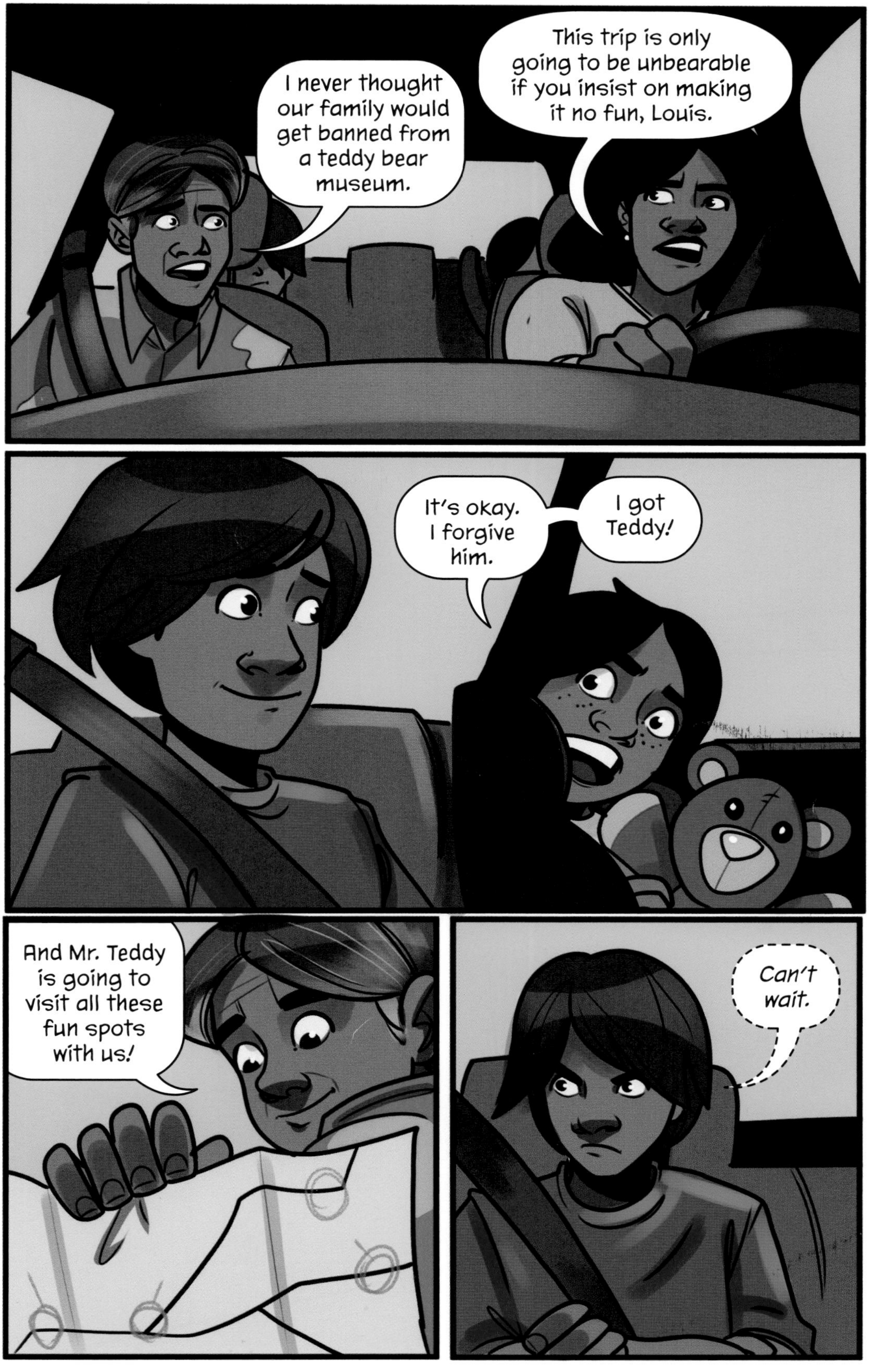
I never thought our family would get banned from a teddy bear museum.
This trip is only going to be unbearable if you insist on making it no fun, Louis.
It's okay. I forgive him.
I got Teddy!
And Mr. Teddy is going to visit all these fun spots with us!
Can't wait.

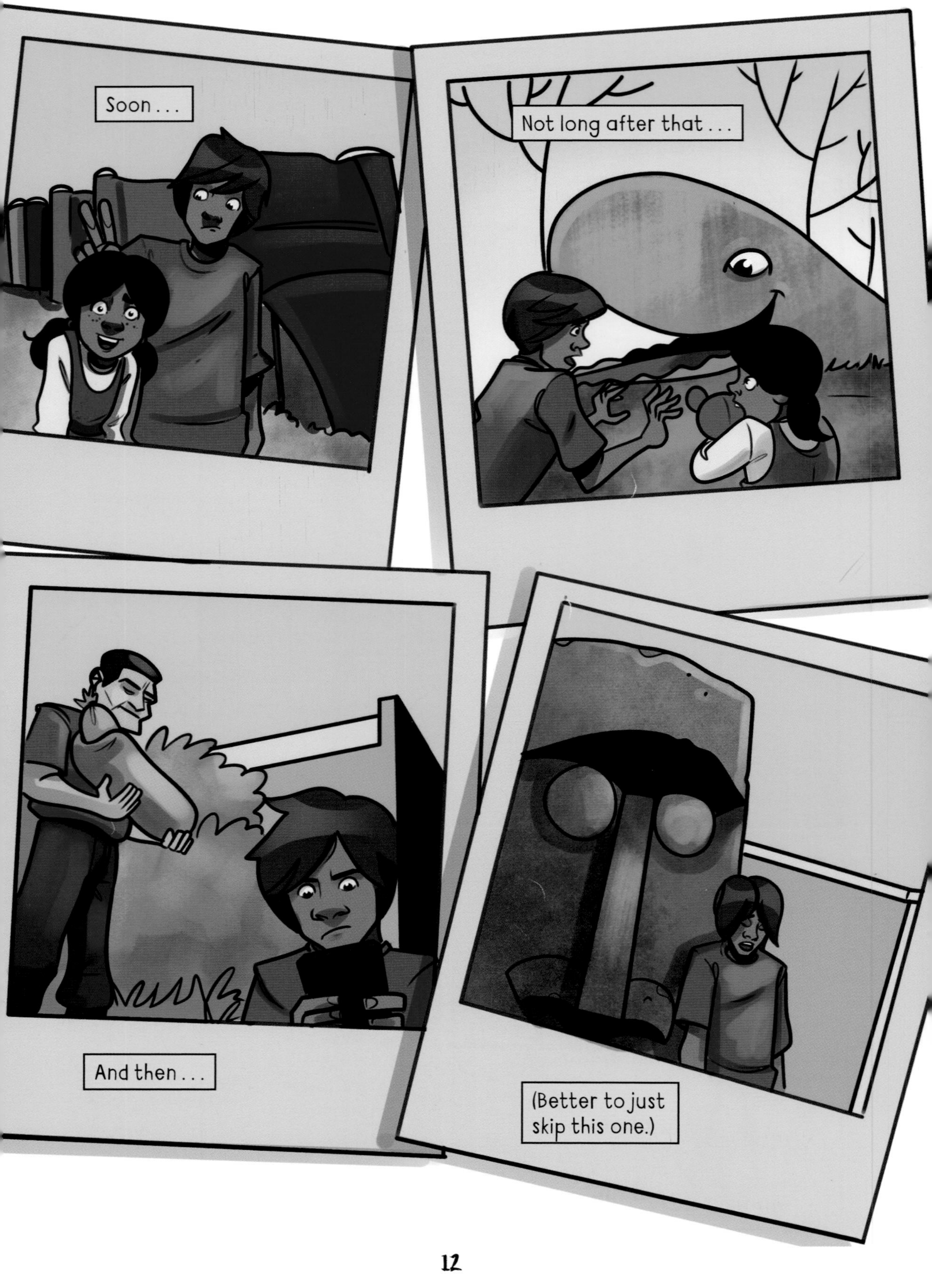

Soon . . .
Not long after that . . .
And then . . .
(Better to just skip this one.)

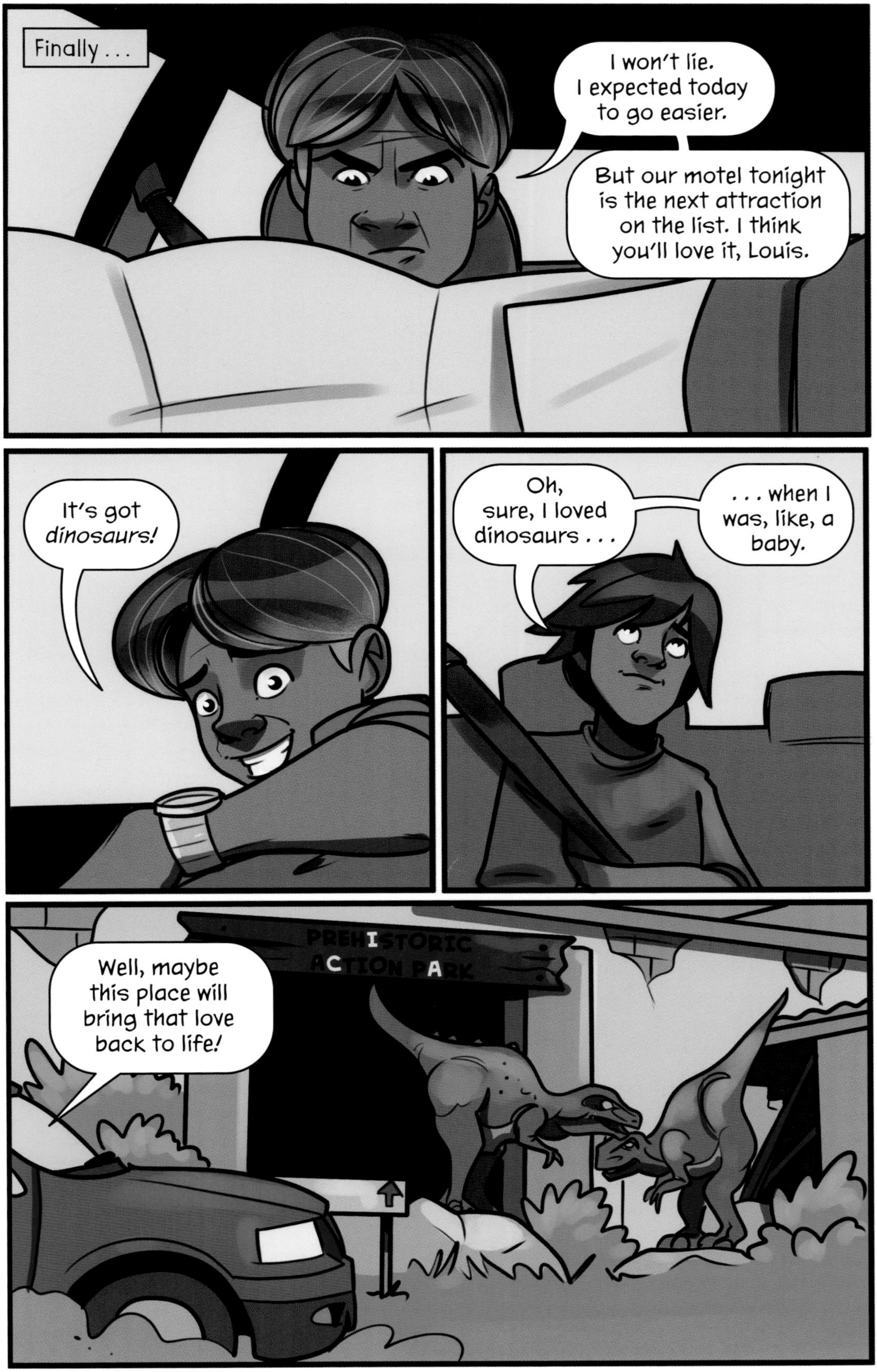
Finally . . .
I won't lie. I expected today to go easier.
But our motel tonight is the next attraction on the list. I think you'll love it, Louis.
It's got *dinosaurs!*
Oh, sure, I loved dinosaurs . . .
. . . when I was, like, a baby.
PREHISTORIC ACTION PARK
Well, maybe this place will bring that love back to life!

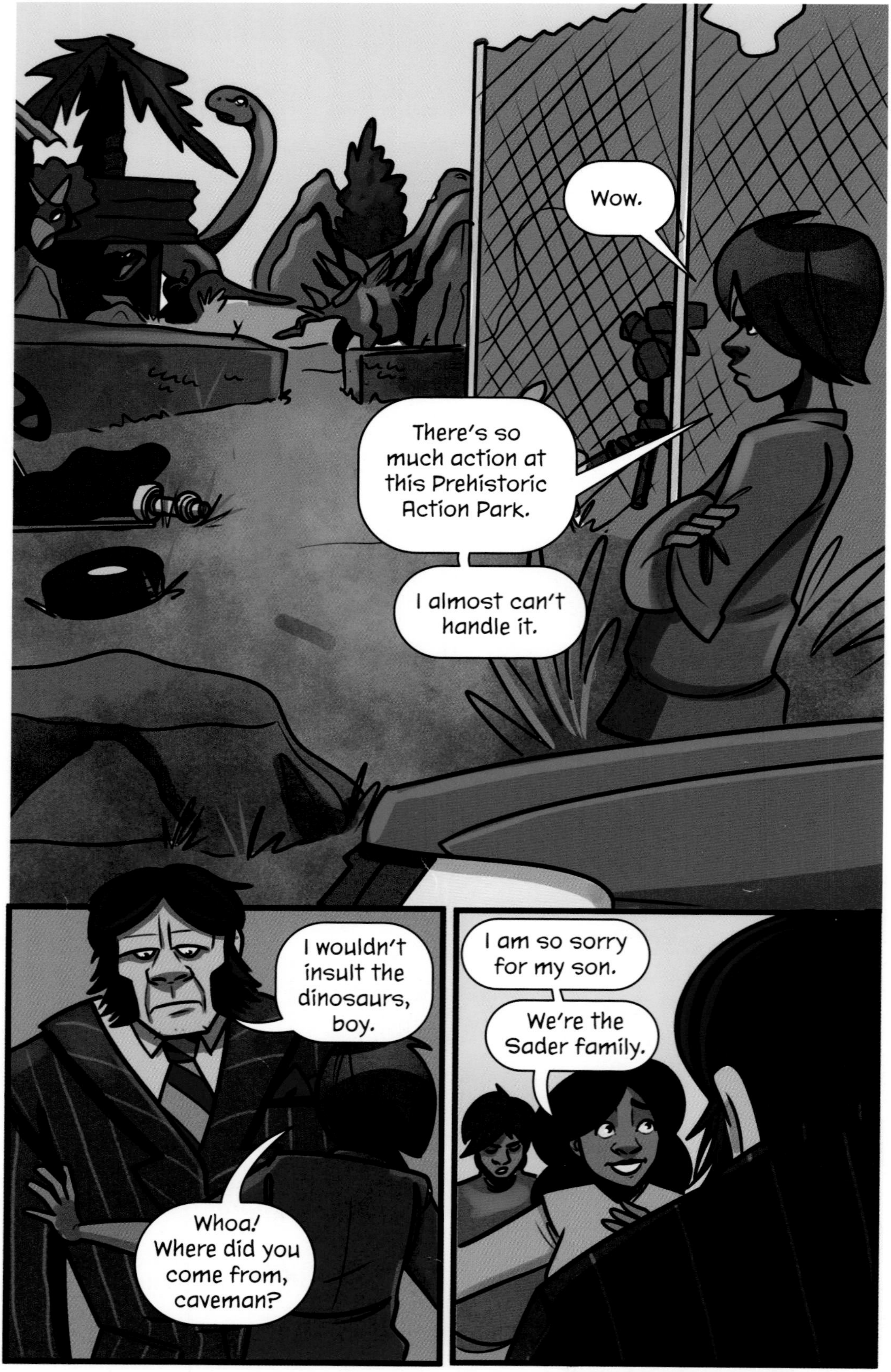
Wow.
There's so much action at this Prehistoric Action Park.
I almost can't handle it.
I wouldn't insult the dinosaurs, boy.
Whoa! Where did you come from, caveman?
I am so sorry for my son.
We're the Sader family.

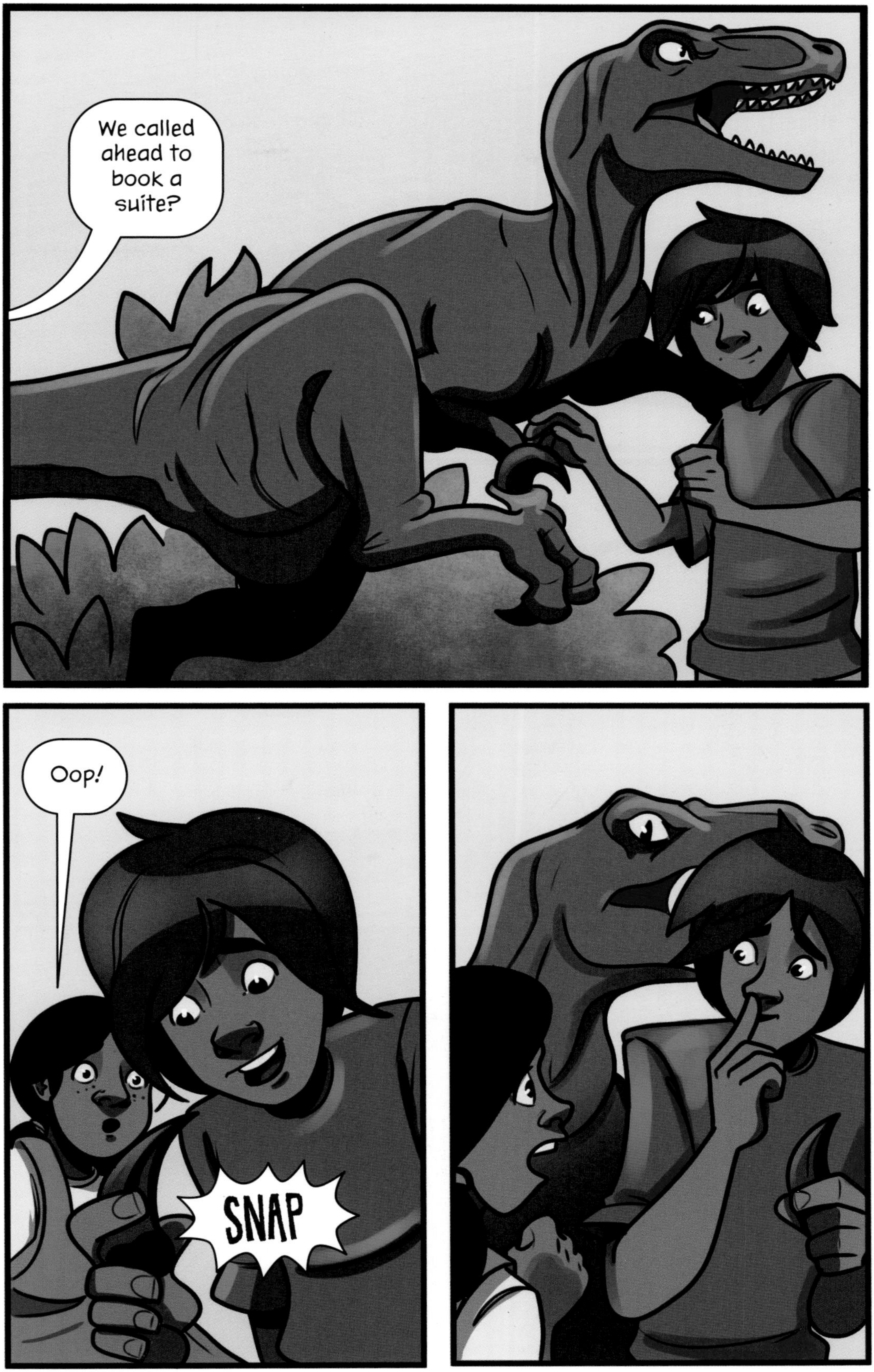
We called ahead to book a suite?
Oop!
SNAP

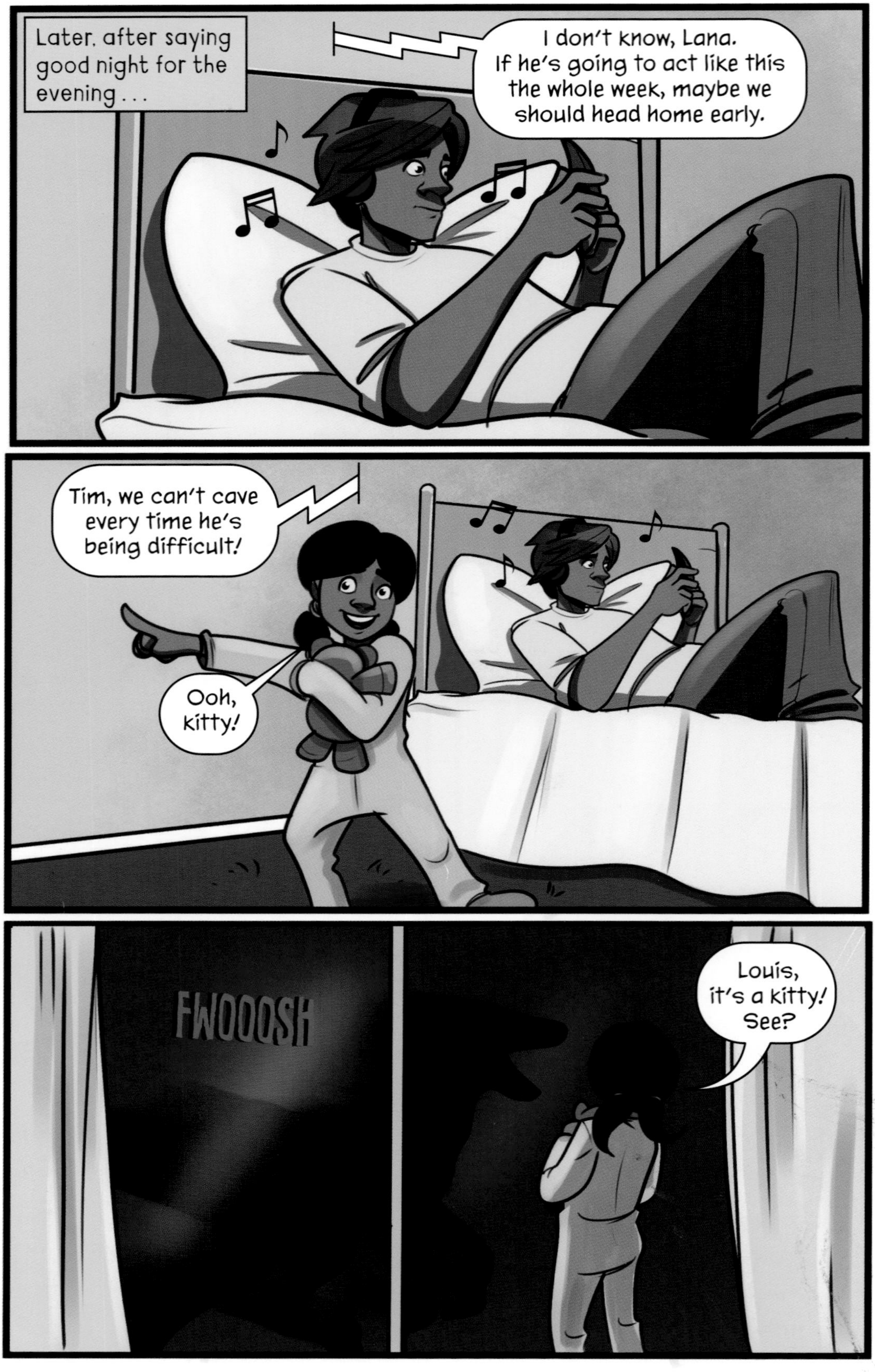
Later, after saying good night for the evening . . .
I don't know, Lana. If he's going to act like this the whole week, maybe we should head home early.
Tim, we can't cave every time he's being difficult!
Ooh, kitty!
FWOOOSH
Louis, it's a kitty! See?

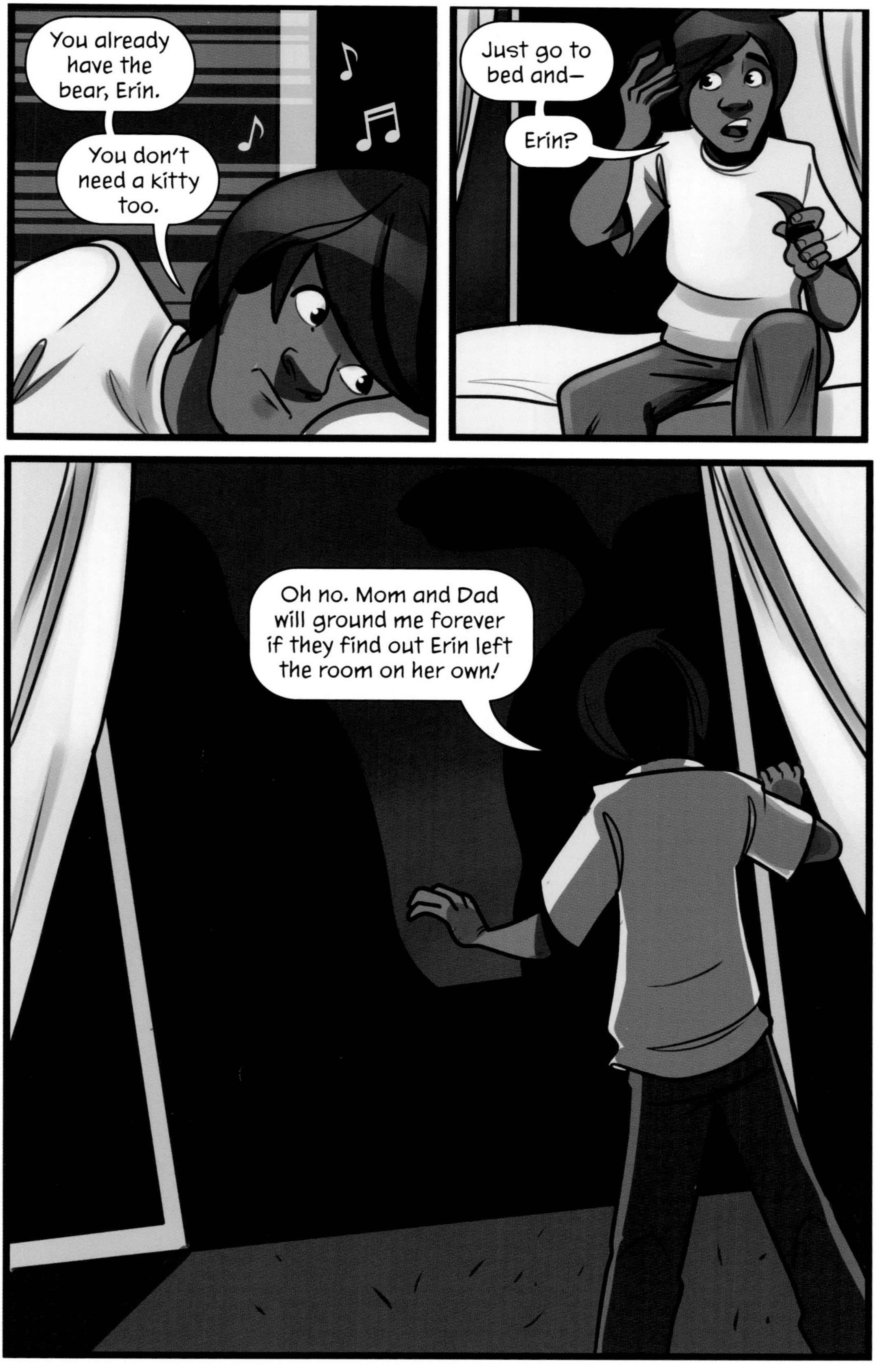
You already have the bear, Erin.
You don't need a kitty too.
Just go to bed and—
Erin?
Oh no. Mom and Dad will ground me forever if they find out Erin left the room on her own!

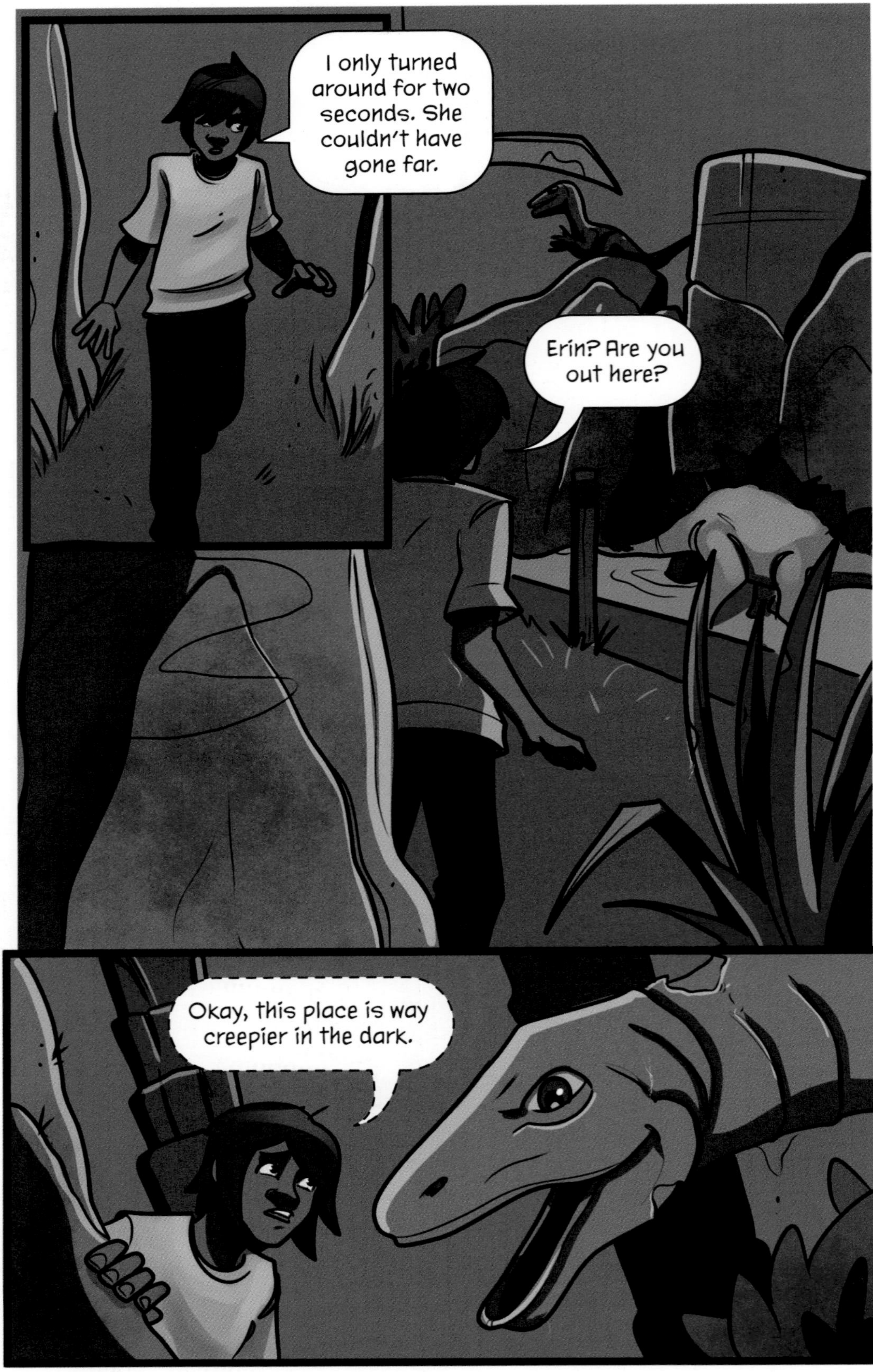
I only turned around for two seconds. She couldn't have gone far.
Erin? Are you out here?
Okay, this place is way creepier in the dark.

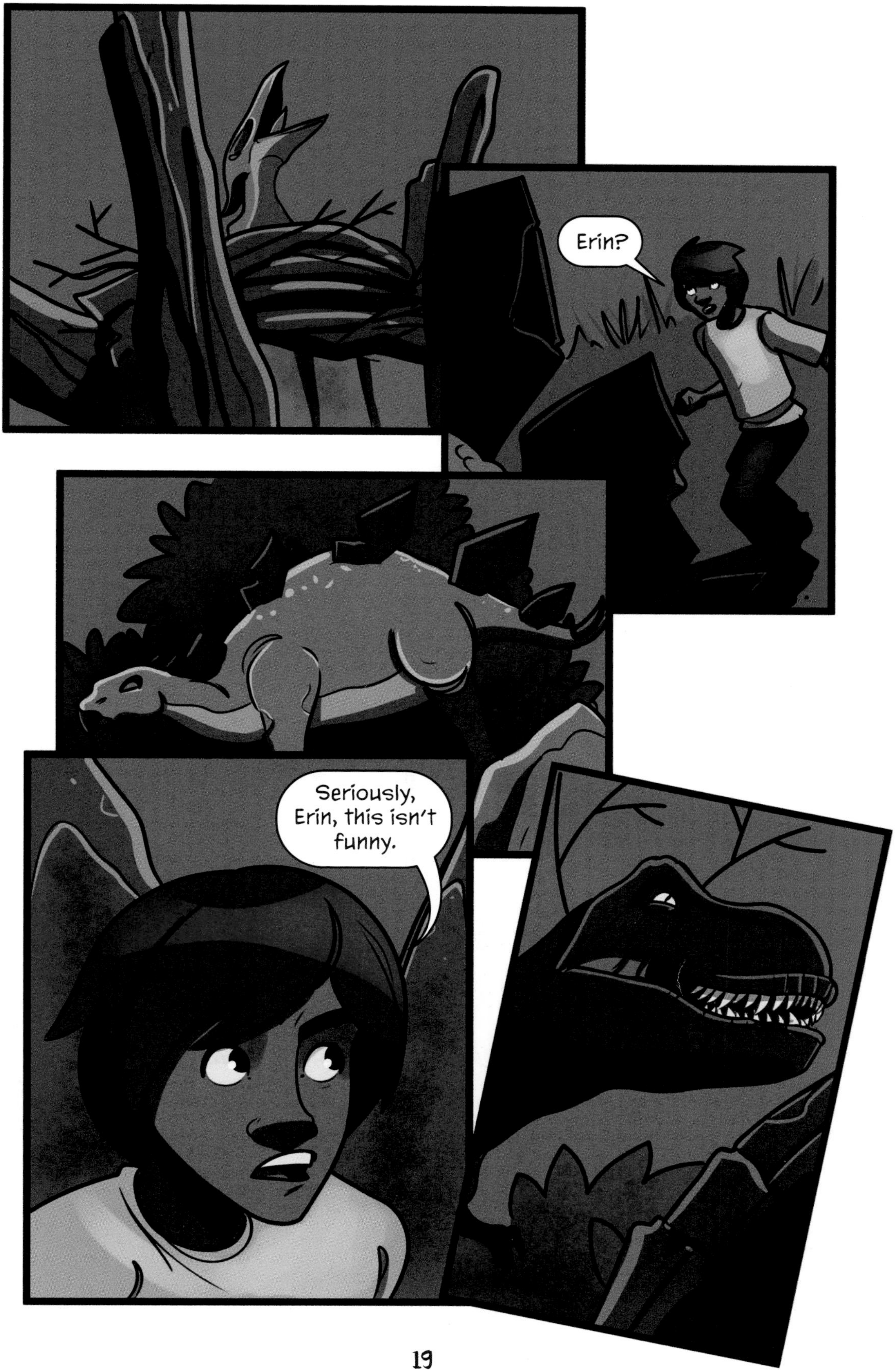
Erin?
Seriously, Erin, this isn't funny.

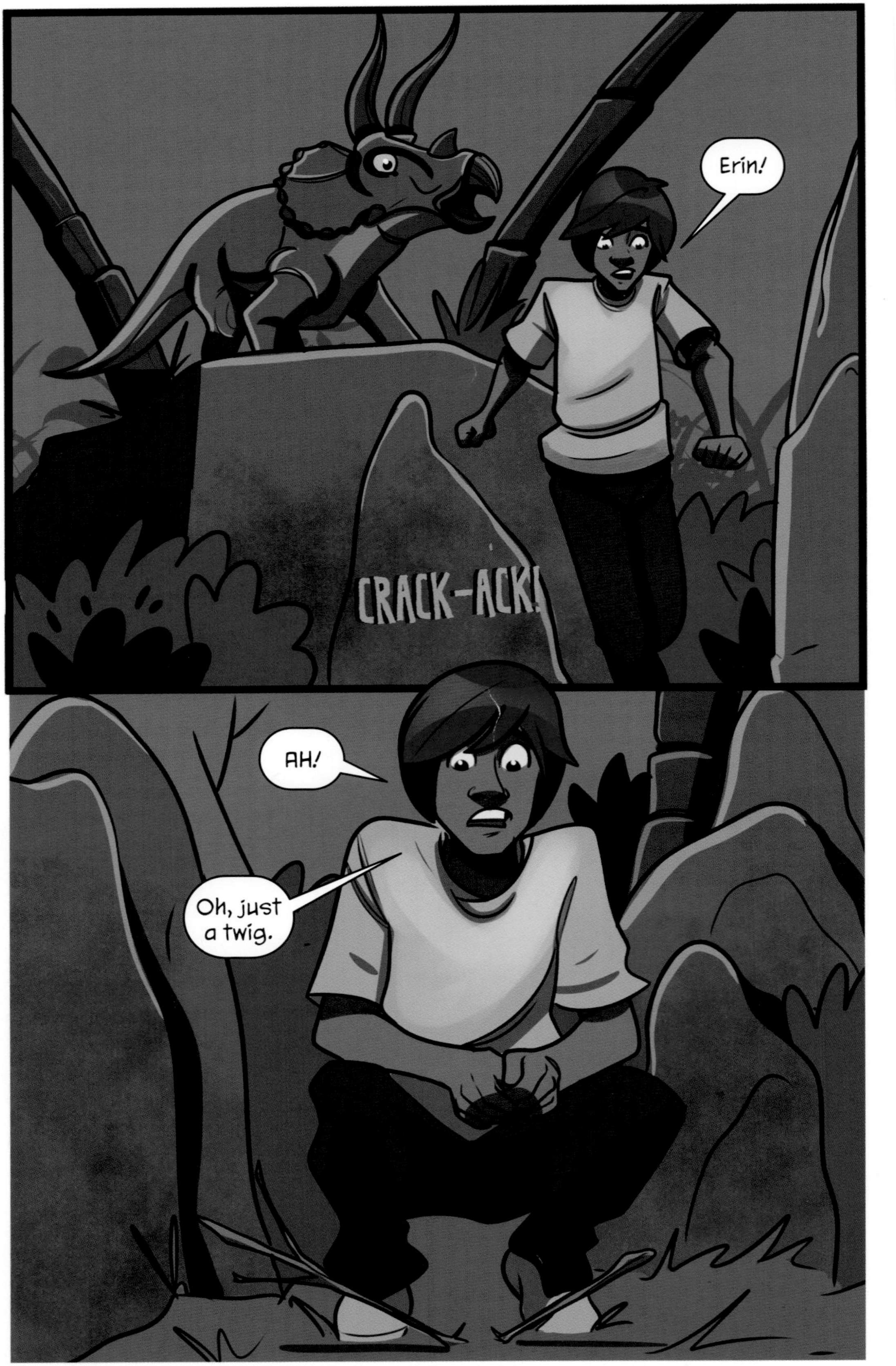
Erin!
CRACK-ACK!
AH!
Oh, just a twig.

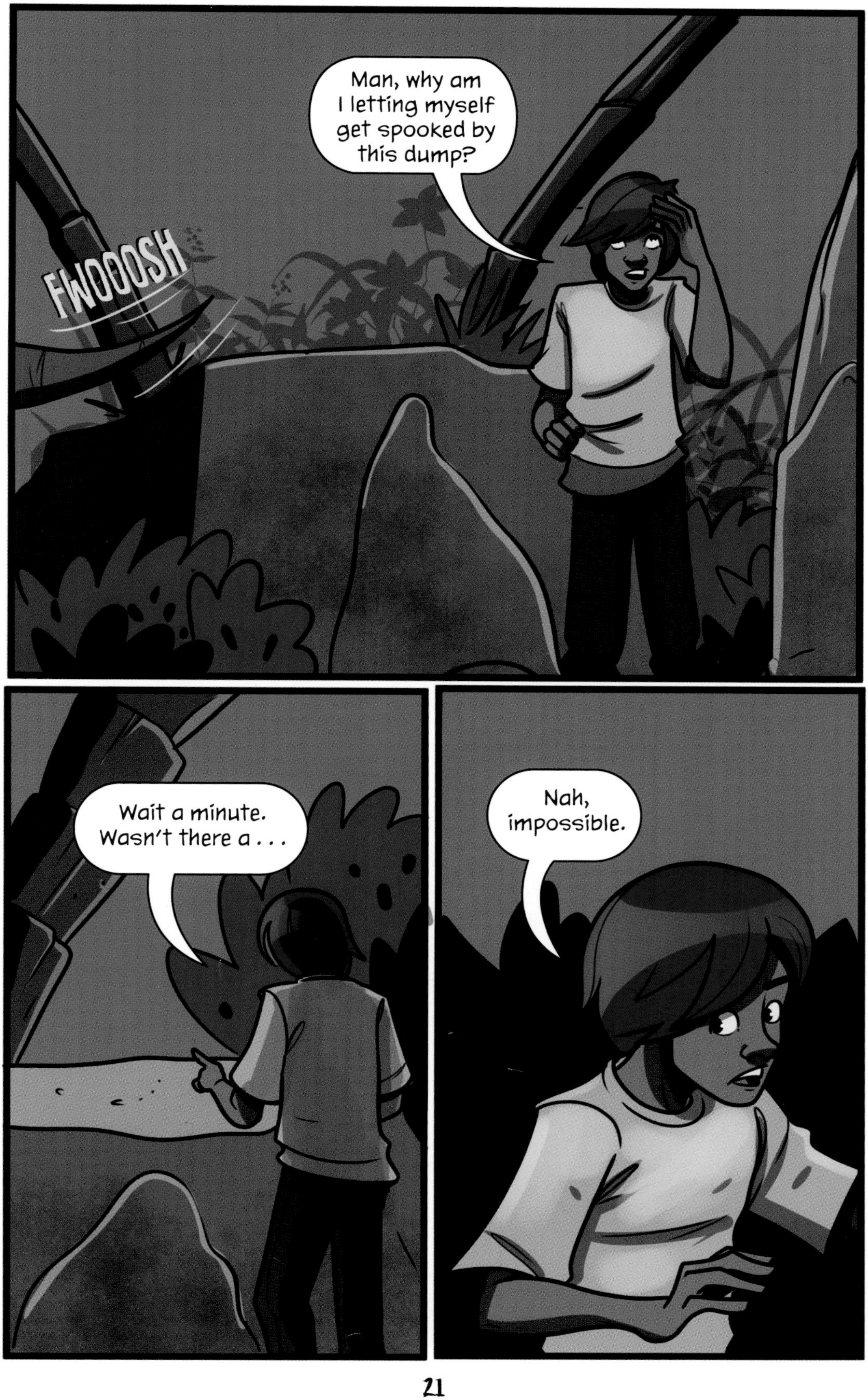
Man, why am I letting myself get spooked by this dump?
FWOOOSH
Wait a minute. Wasn't there a . . .
Nah, impossible.

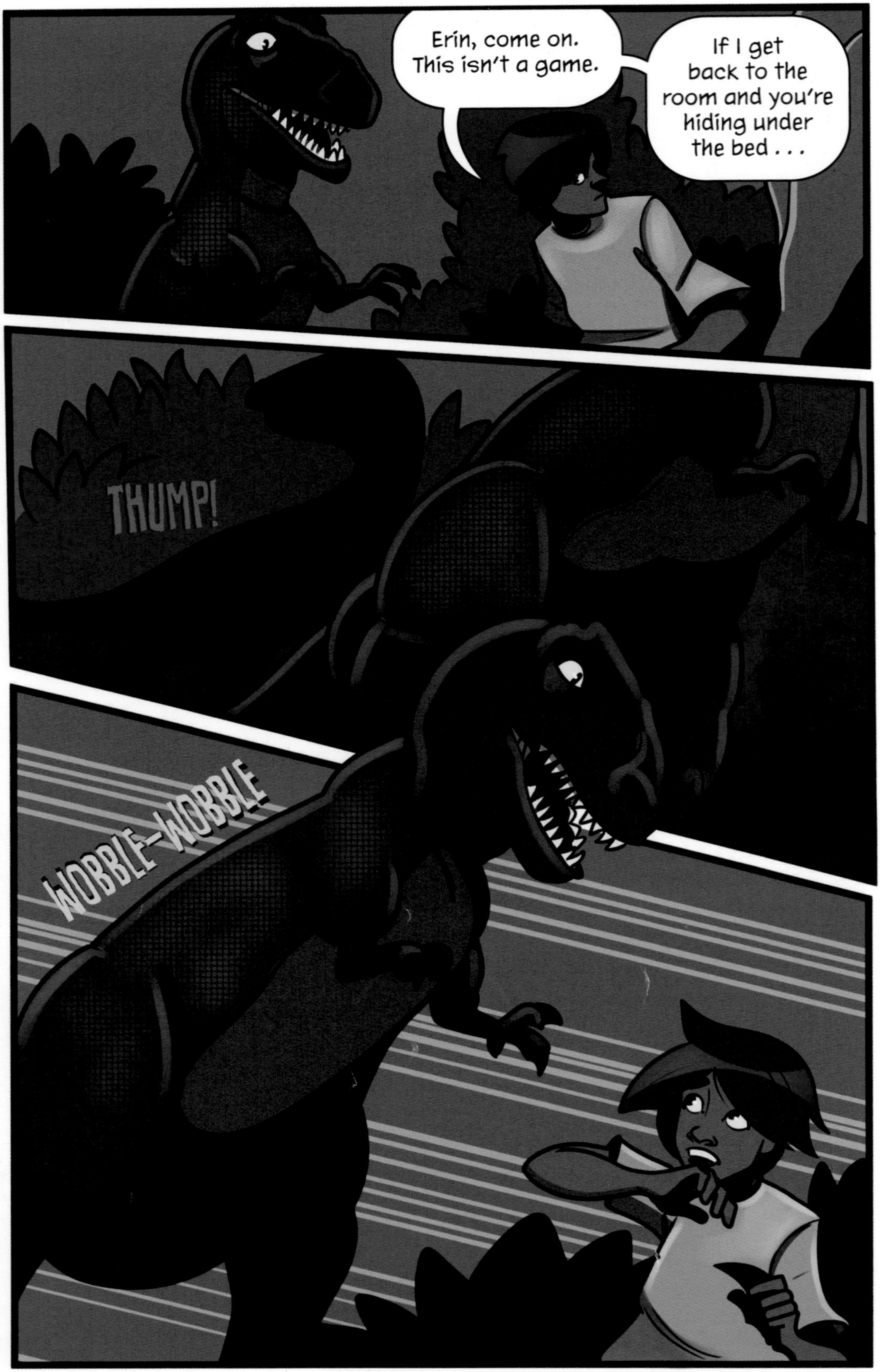
Erin, come on. This isn't a game.
If I get back to the room and you're hiding under the bed . . .
THUMP!
WOBBLE-WOBBLE

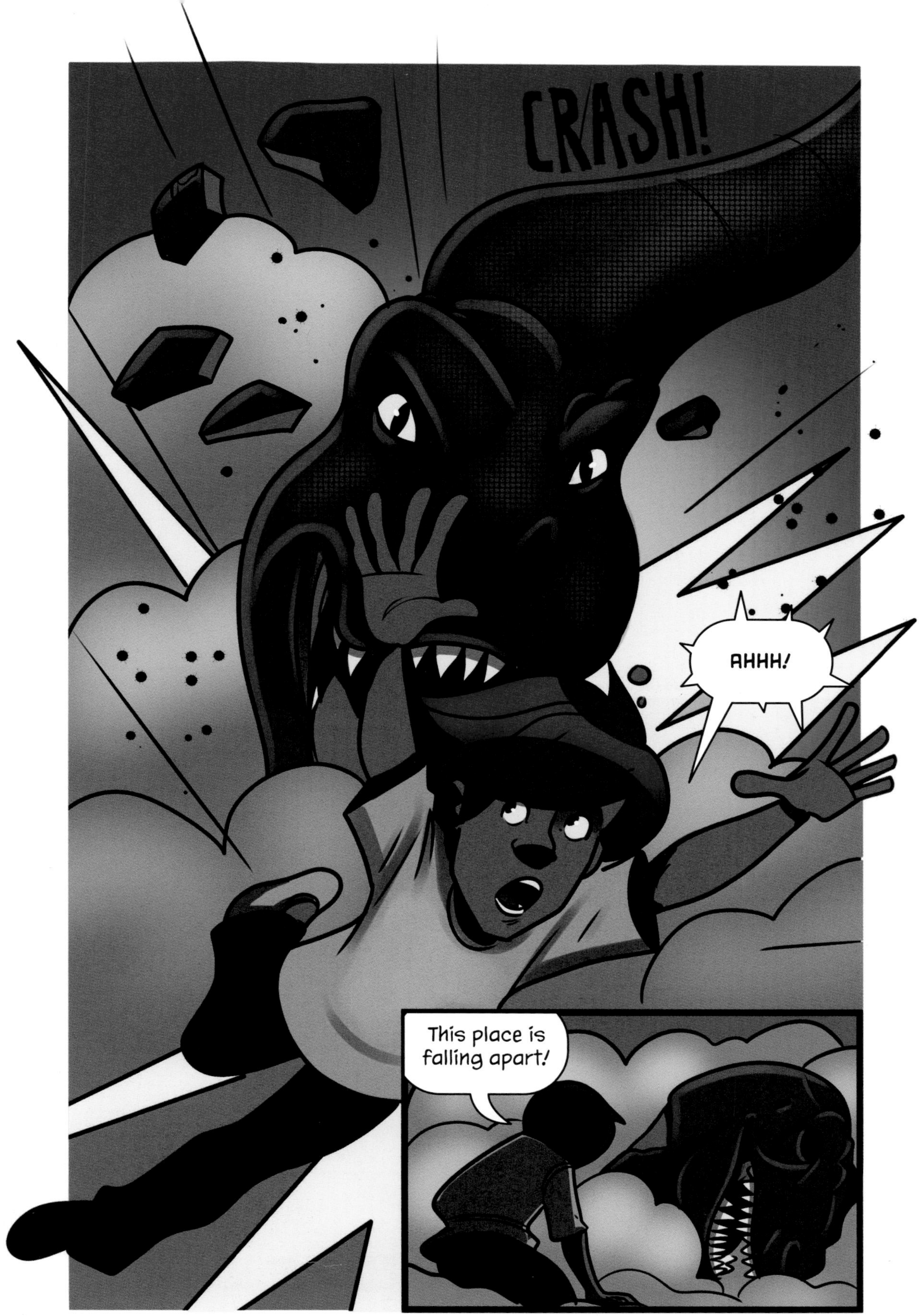
CRASH!
AHHH!
This place is falling apart!

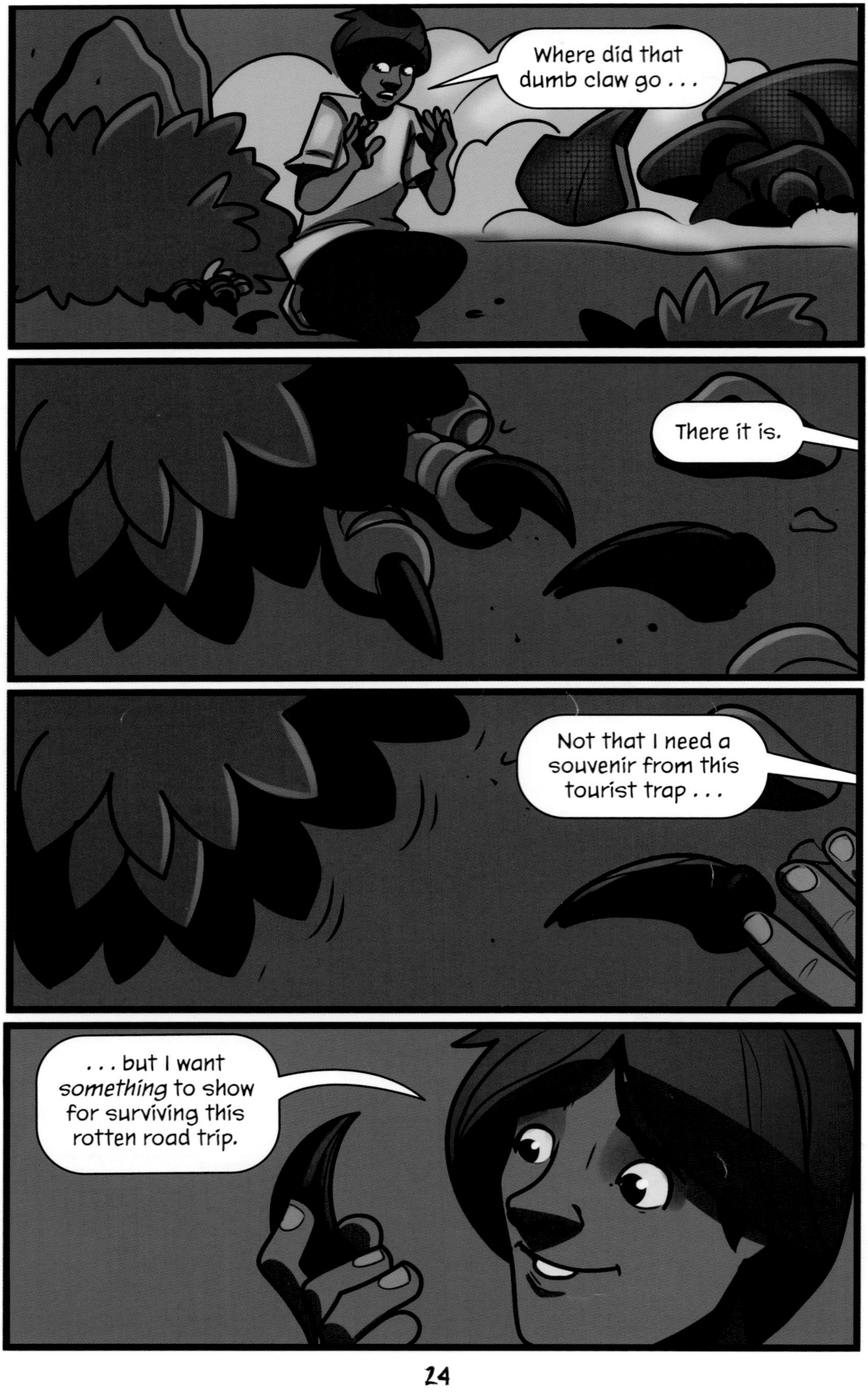
Where did that dumb claw go . . .
There it is.
Not that I need a souvenir from this tourist trap . . .
. . . but I want *something* to show for surviving this rotten road trip.

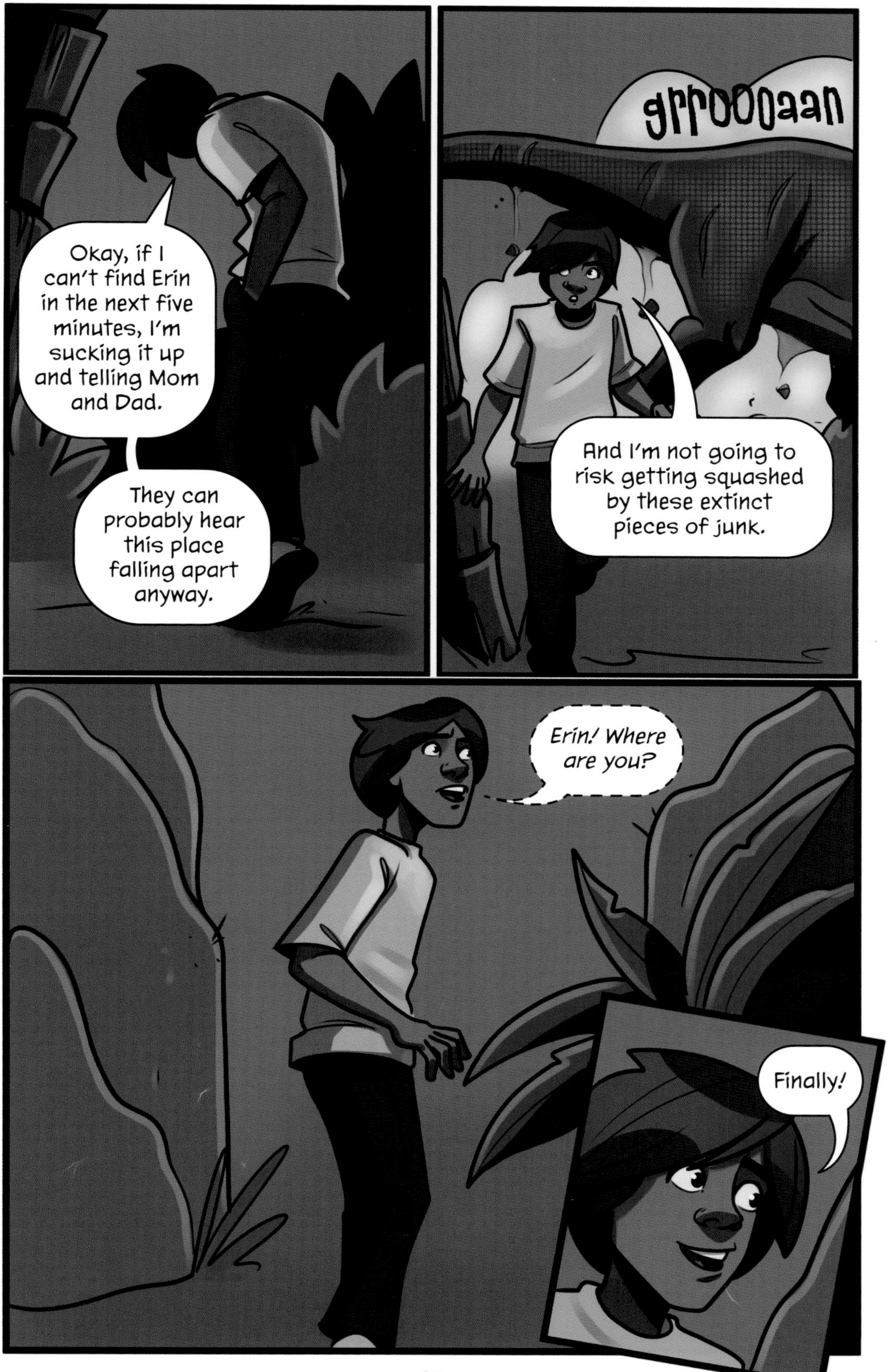
Okay, if I can't find Erin in the next five minutes, I'm sucking it up and telling Mom and Dad.
They can probably hear this place falling apart anyway.
grrooooaan
And I'm not going to risk getting squashed by these extinct pieces of junk.
Erin! Where are you?
Finally!

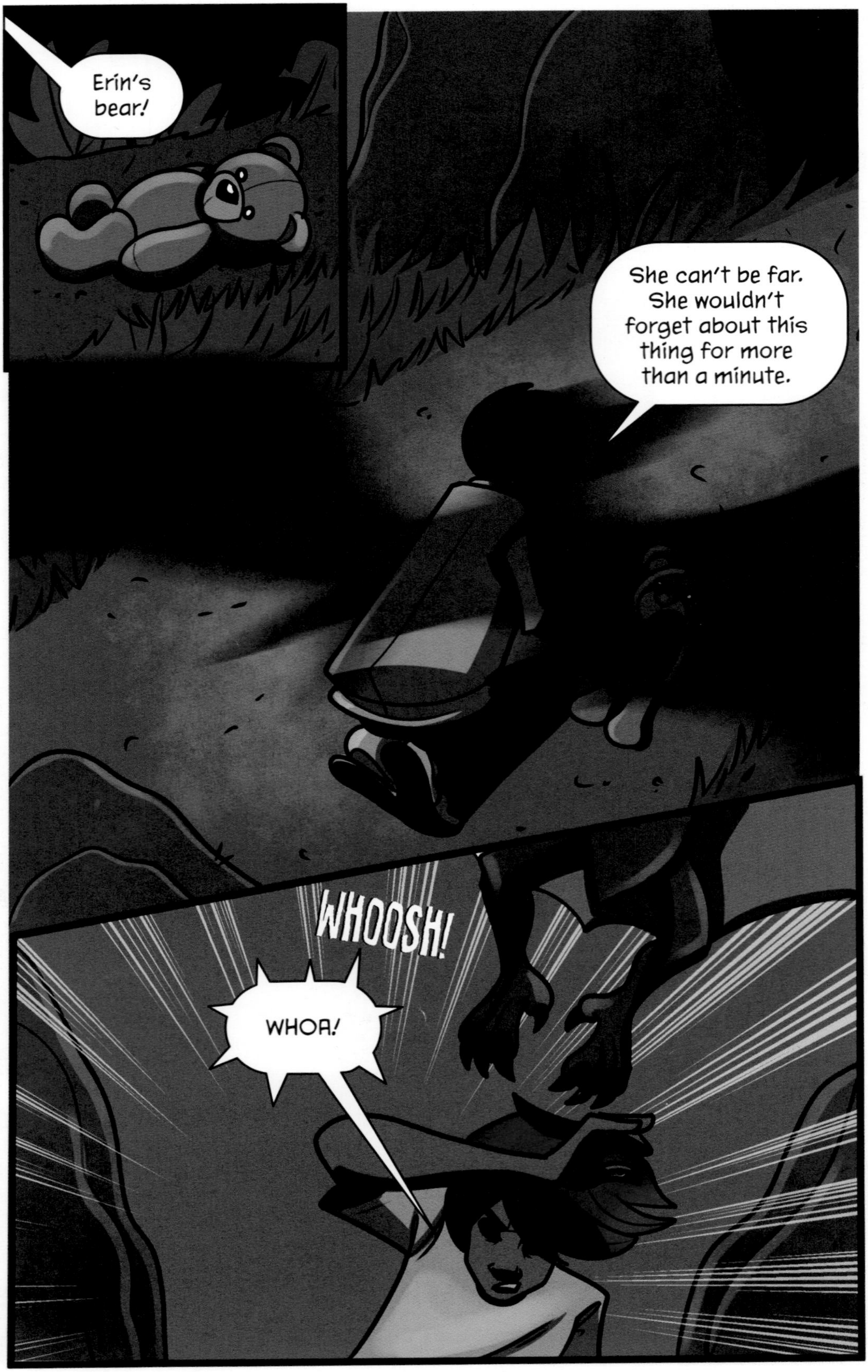
Erin's bear!
She can't be far. She wouldn't forget about this thing for more than a minute.
WHOOSH!
WHOA!

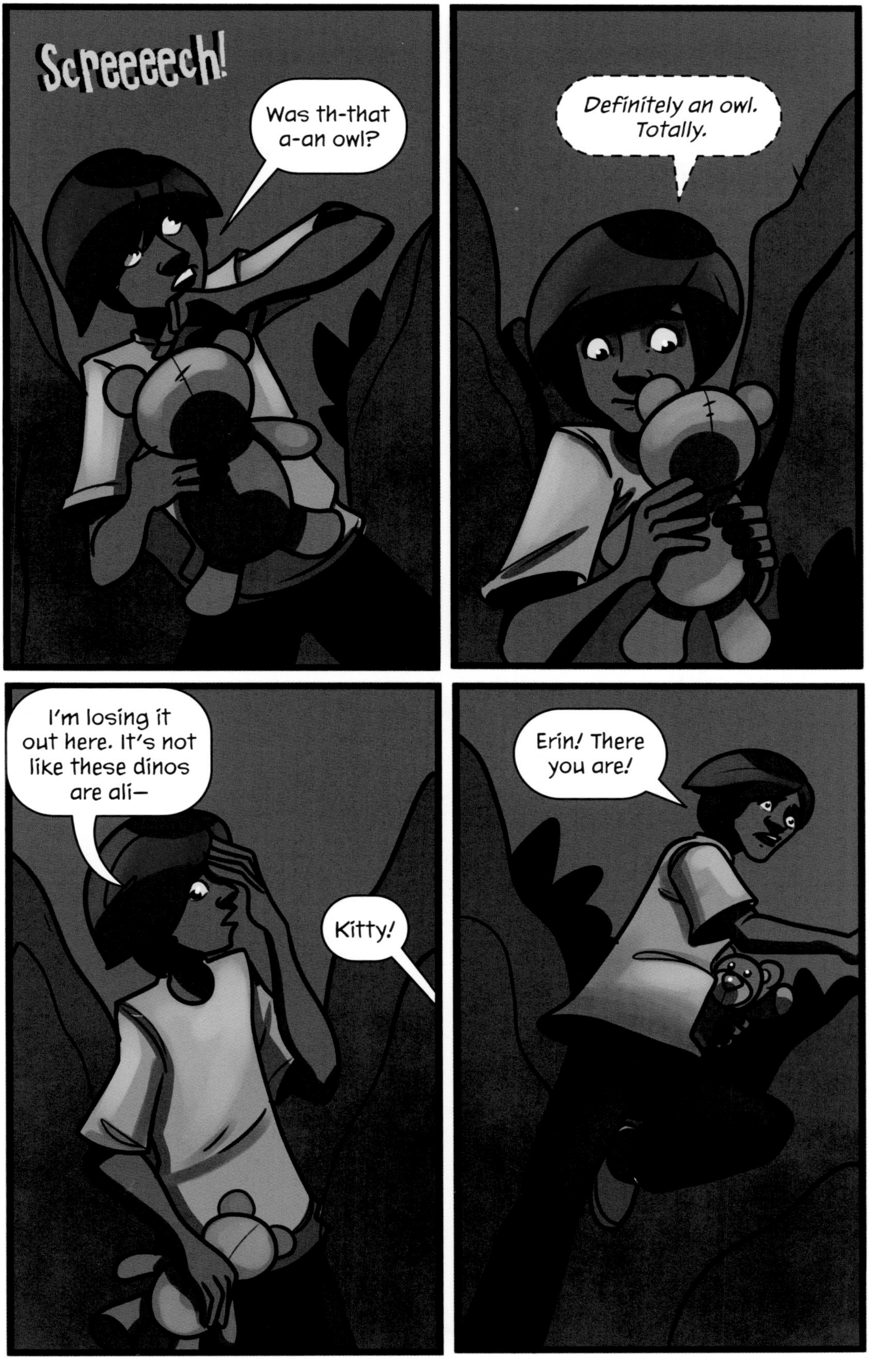
Screeeech!
Was th-that a-an owl?
Definitely an owl. Totally.
I'm losing it out here. It's not like these dinos are ali—
Kitty!
Erin! There you are!

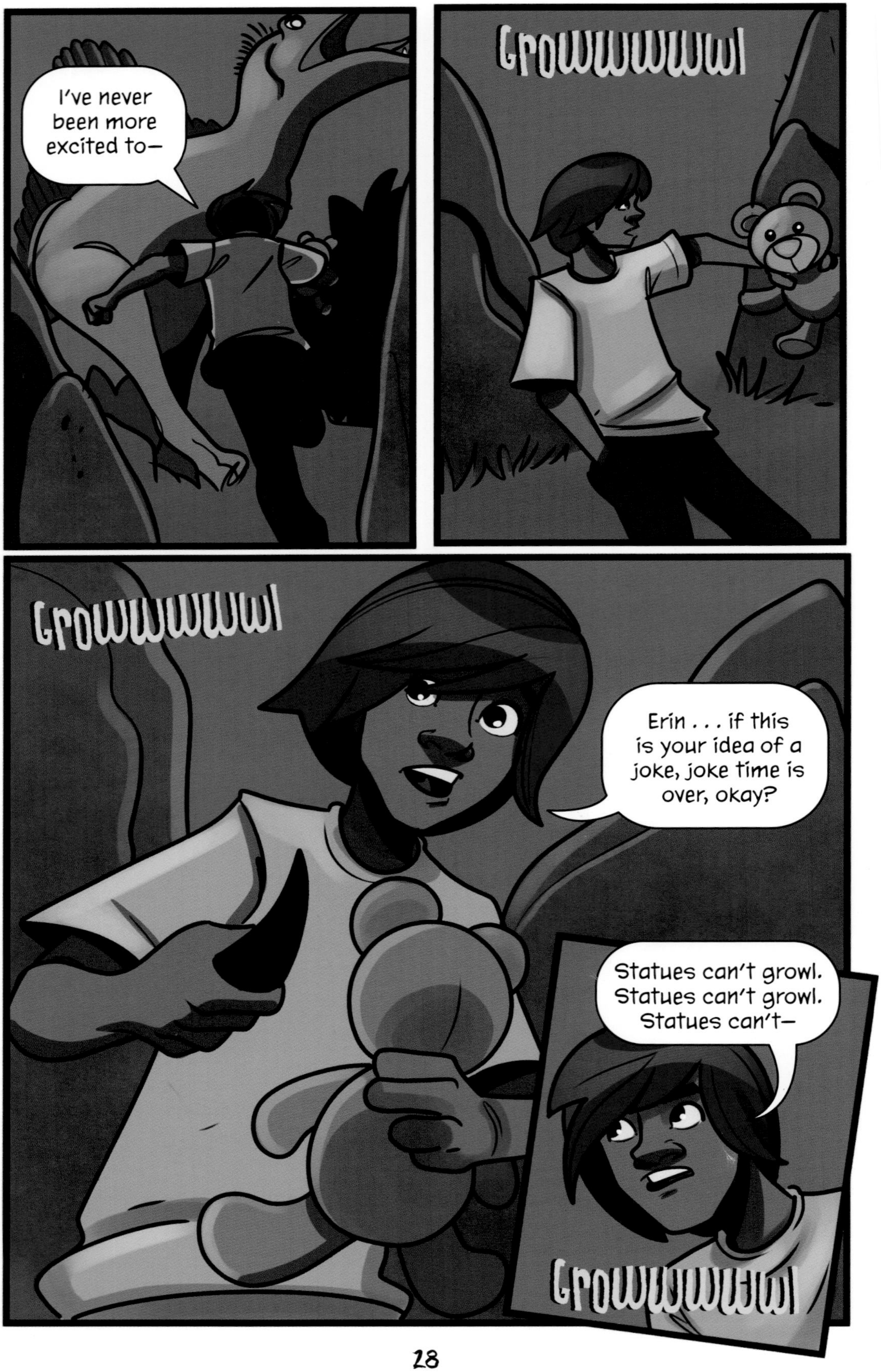

I've never been more excited to—
GROWWWWWL
GROWWWWWL
Erin . . . if this is your idea of a joke, joke time is over, okay?
Statues can't growl. Statues can't growl. Statues can't—
GROWWWWWWL

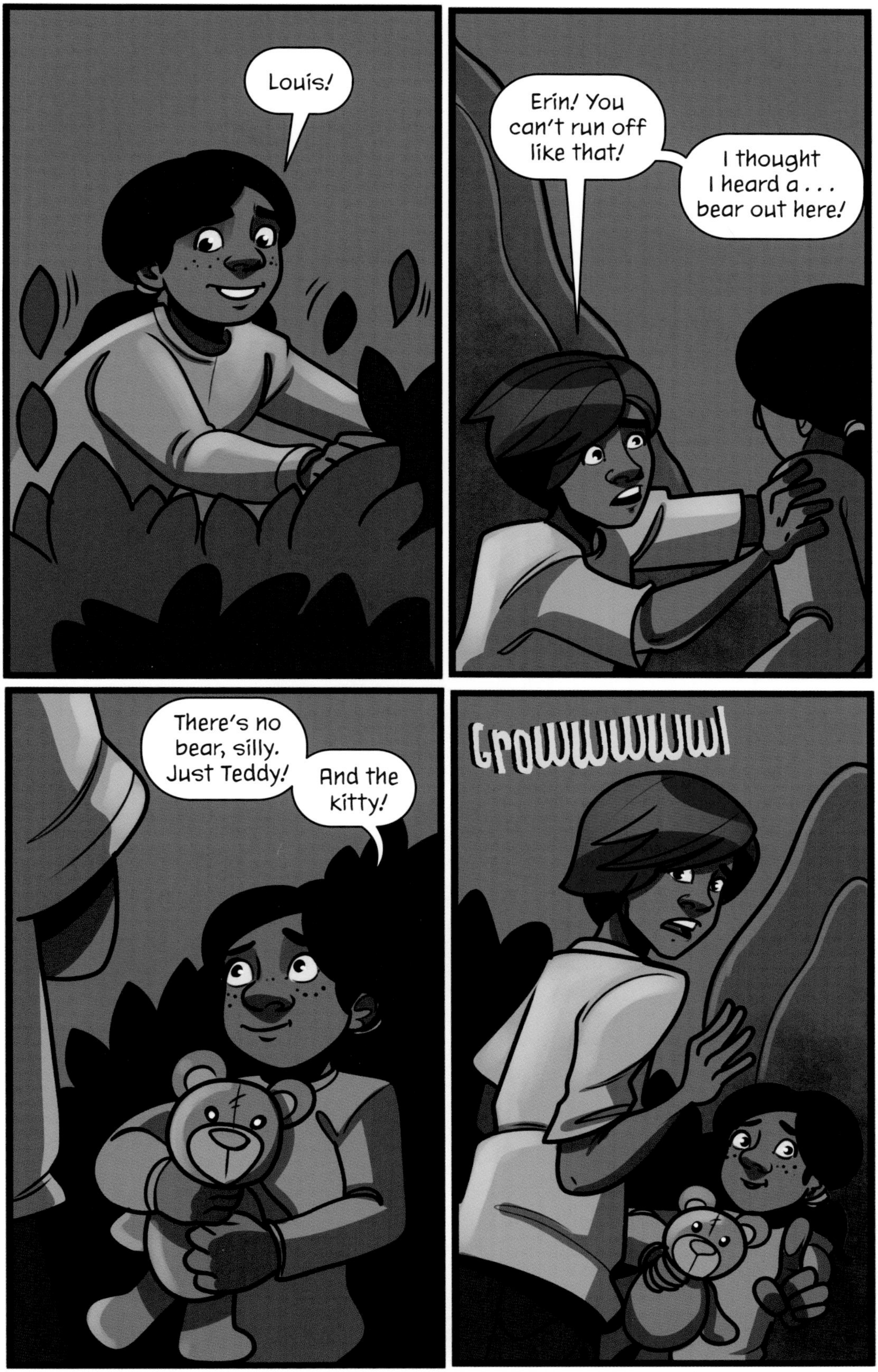
Louis!
Erin! You can't run off like that!
I thought I heard a . . . bear out here!
There's no bear, silly. Just Teddy!
And the kitty!
GROWWWWWWL

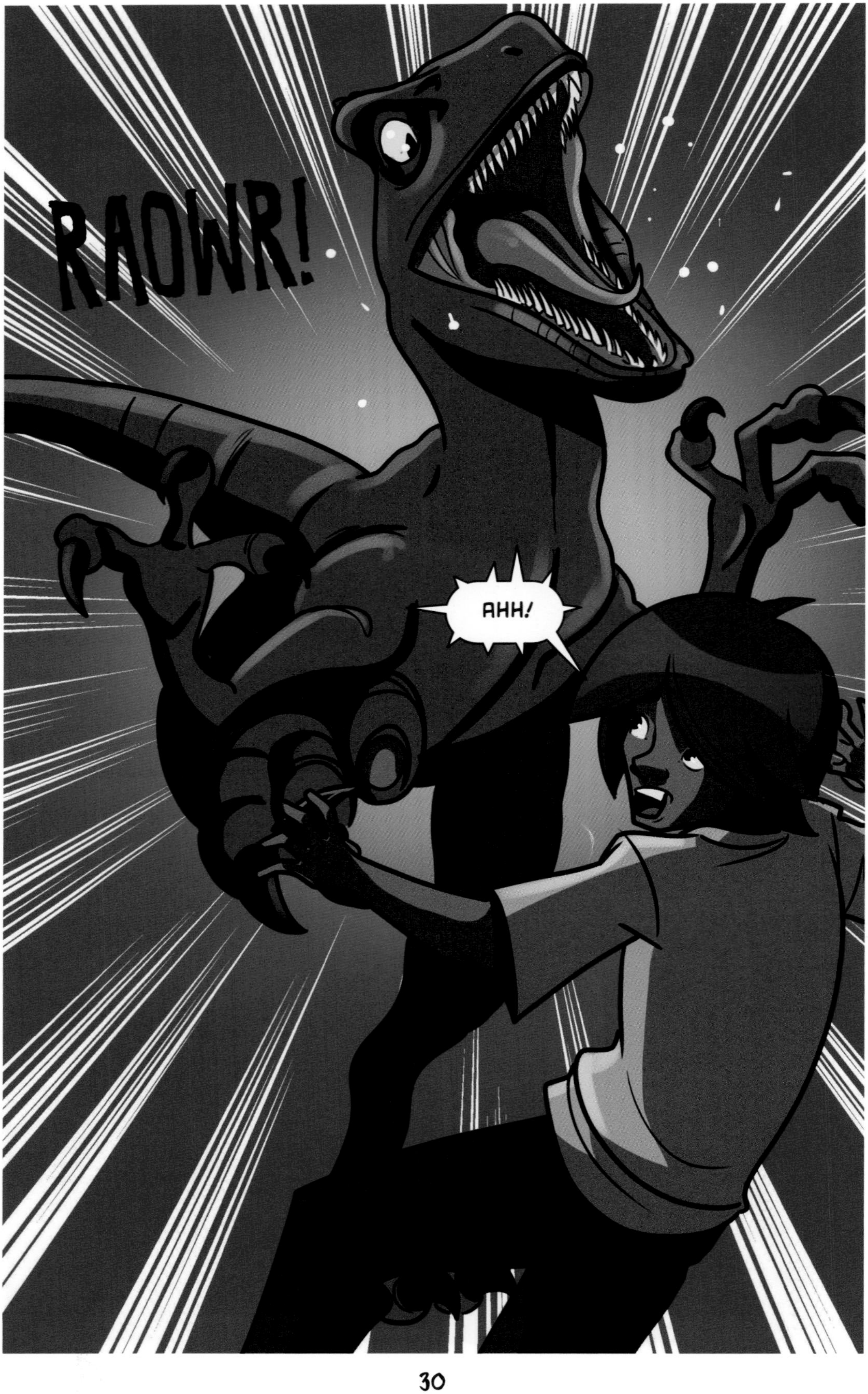
RAOWR!
AHH!

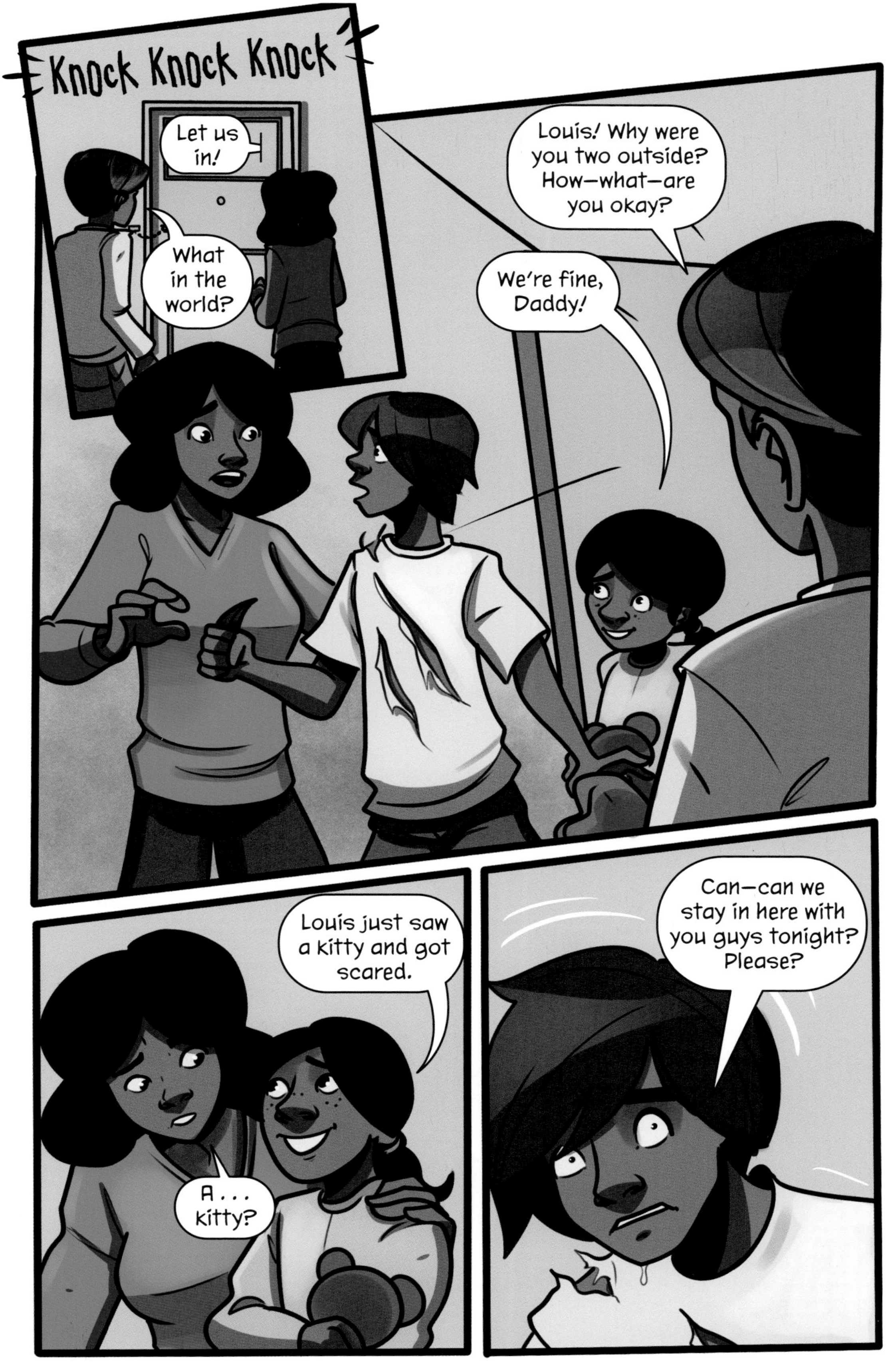
Knock Knock Knock
Let us in!
What in the world?
Louis! Why were you two outside? How—what—are you okay?
We're fine, Daddy!
Louis just saw a kitty and got scared.
A . . . kitty?
Can—can we stay in here with you guys tonight? Please?

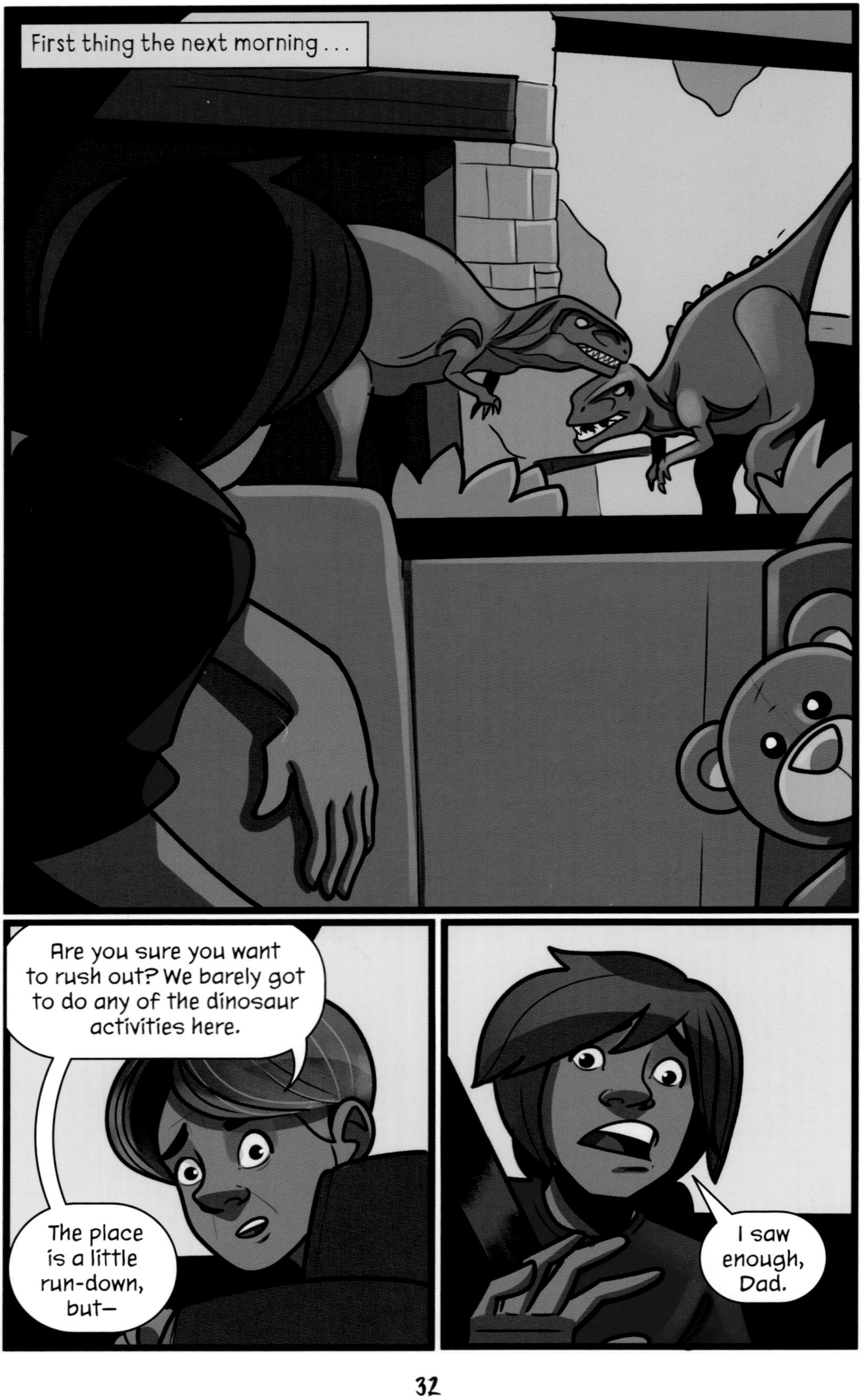
First thing the next morning . . .
Are you sure you want to rush out? We barely got to do any of the dinosaur activities here.
The place is a little run-down, but—
I saw enough, Dad.

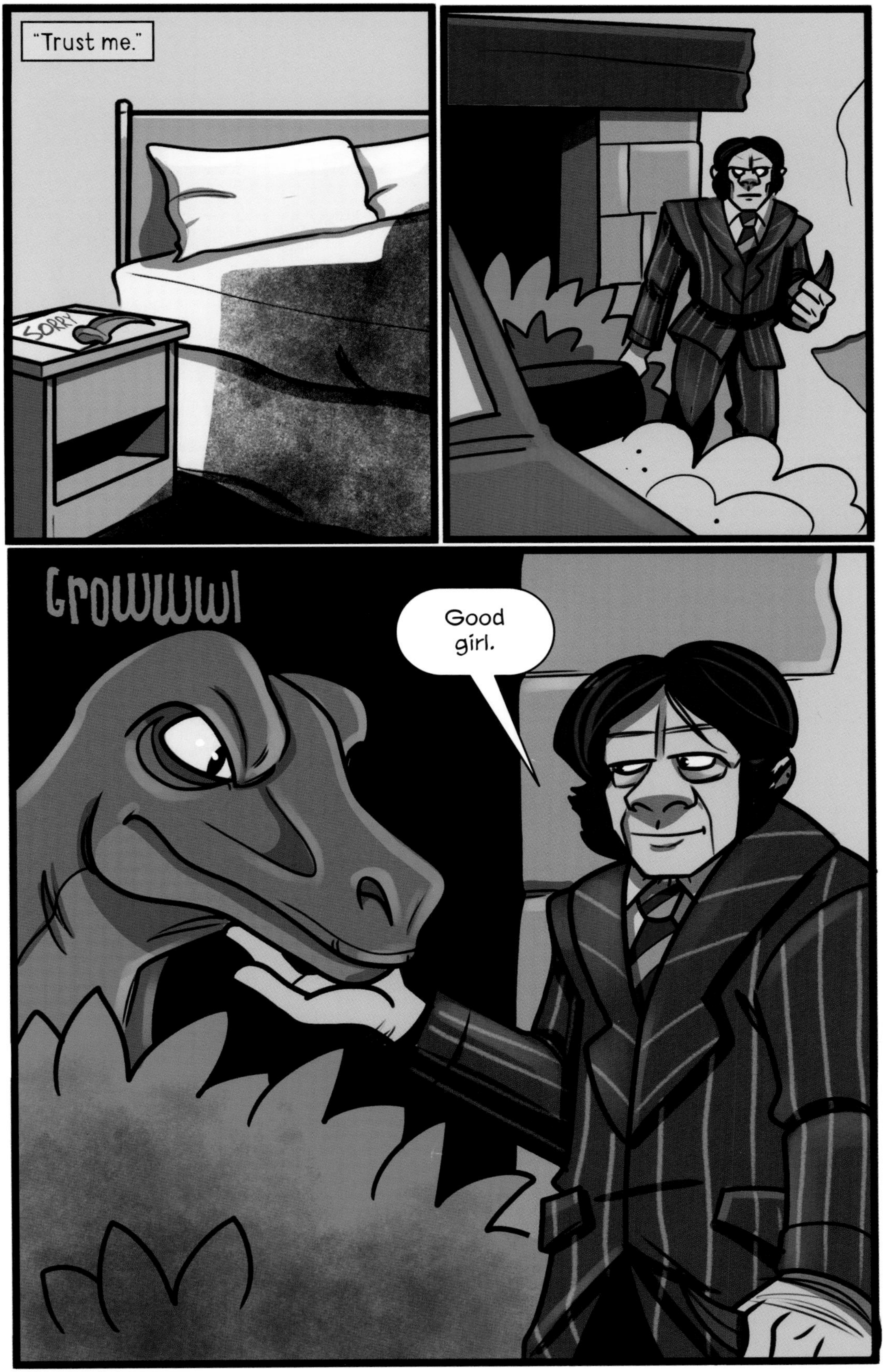
"Trust me."
SORRY
Growwwl
Good girl.

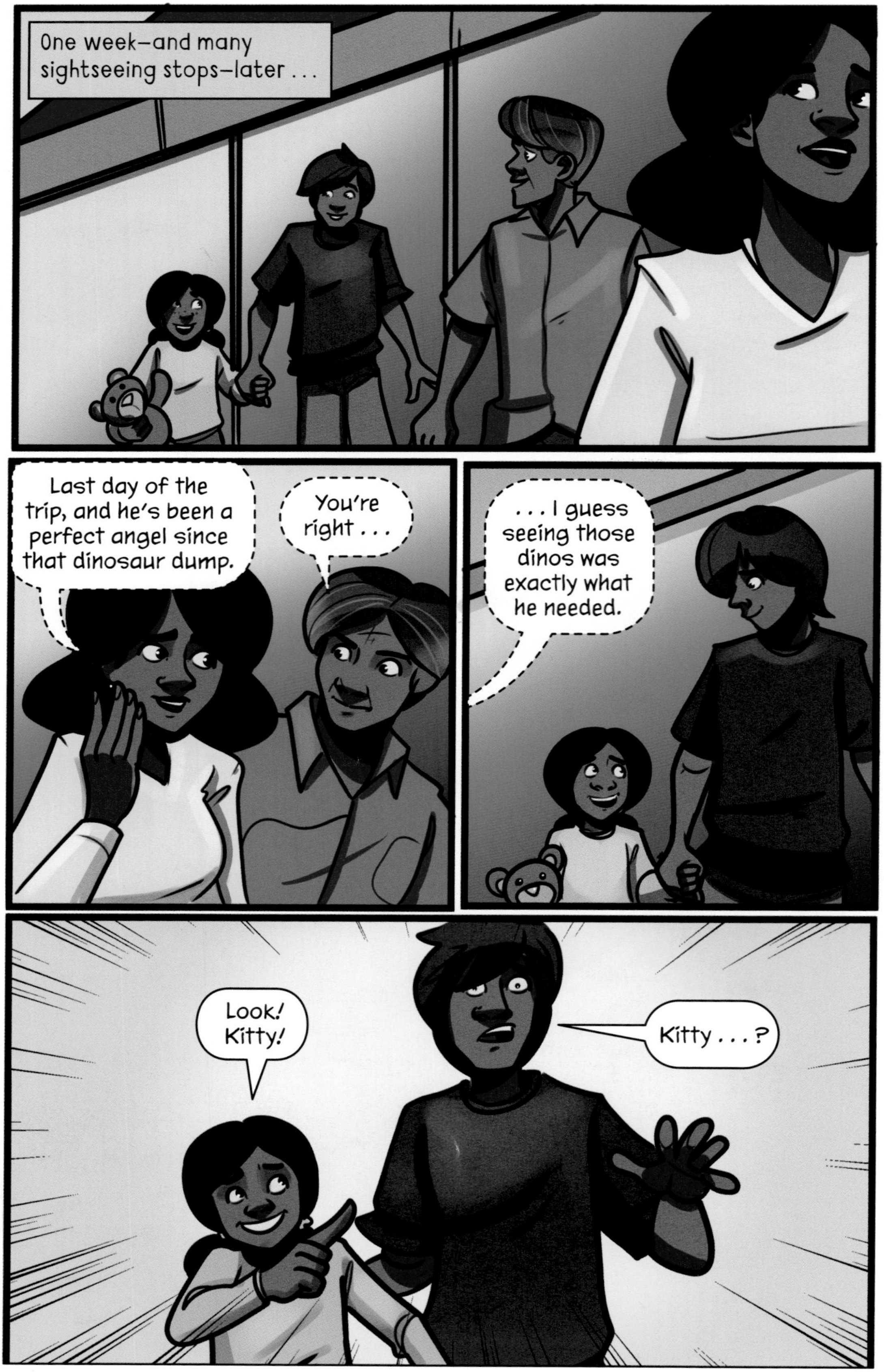
One week—and many sightseeing stops—later . . .
Last day of the trip, and he's been a perfect angel since that dinosaur dump.
You're right . . .
. . . I guess seeing those dinos was exactly what he needed.
Look! Kitty!
Kitty . . . ?

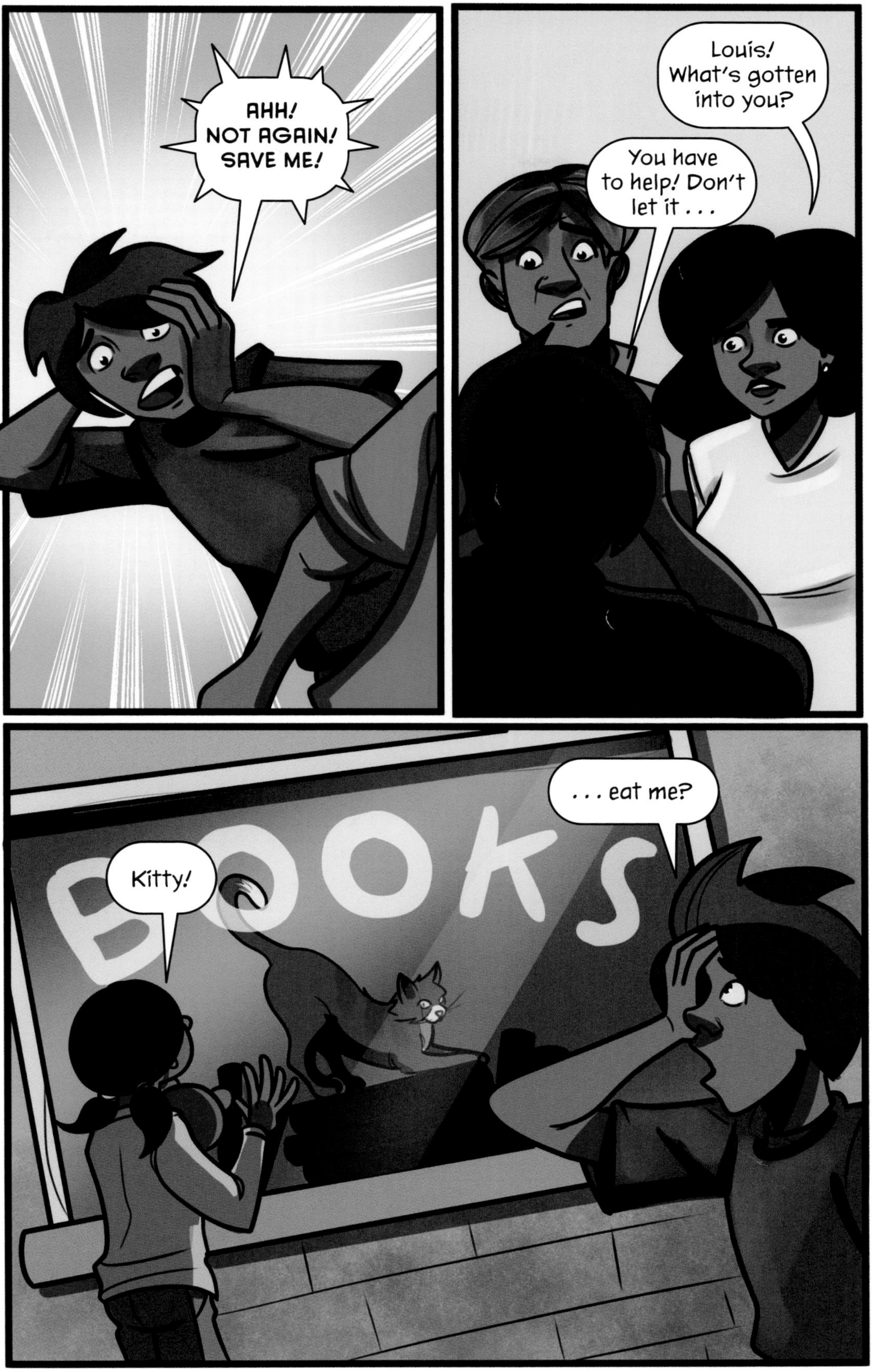
AHH! NOT AGAIN! SAVE ME!
Louis! What's gotten into you?
You have to help! Don't let it . . .
. . . eat me?
Kitty!
BOOKS

LOOK CLOSER

1. Flip through the story and find at least three moments that hint Prehistoric Action Park isn't a normal tourist stop. Be sure to look at both the text and art.

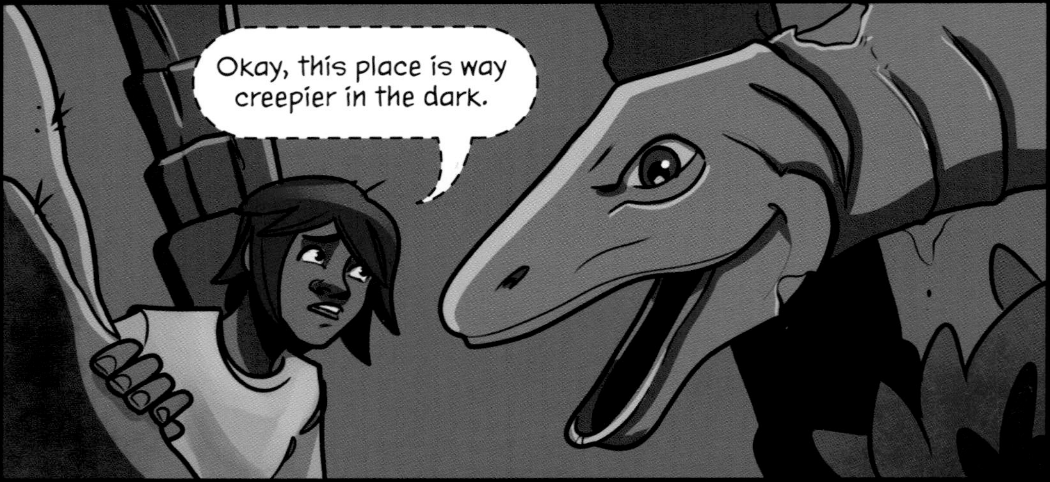
Okay, this place is way creepier in the dark.

2. Why do you think the illustrator used a bright red background here? What feeling does it create?

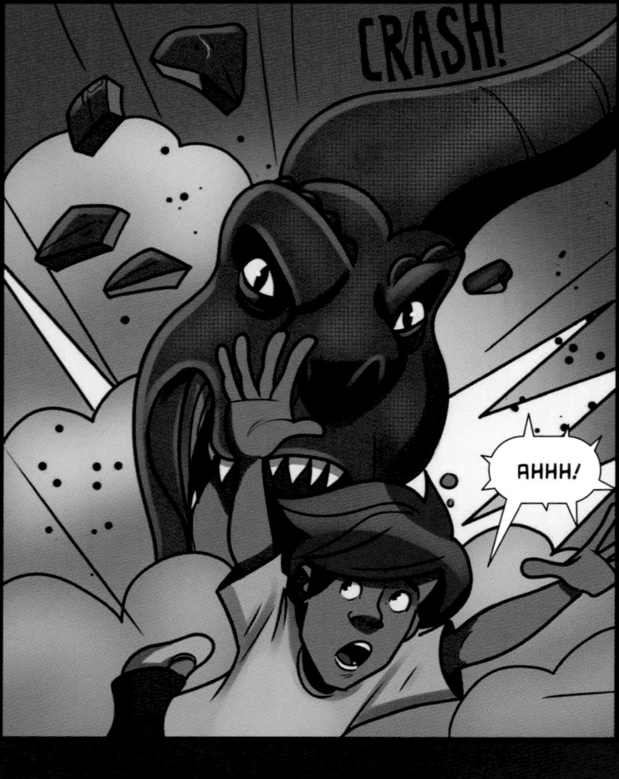
CRASH!
AHHH!

3. What was the "kitty" that Erin kept seeing? Were you surprised by what it really was? Why or why not?

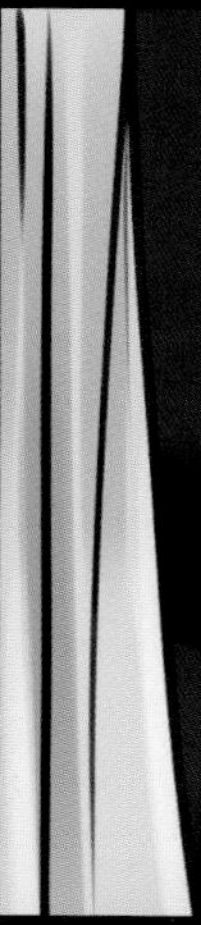

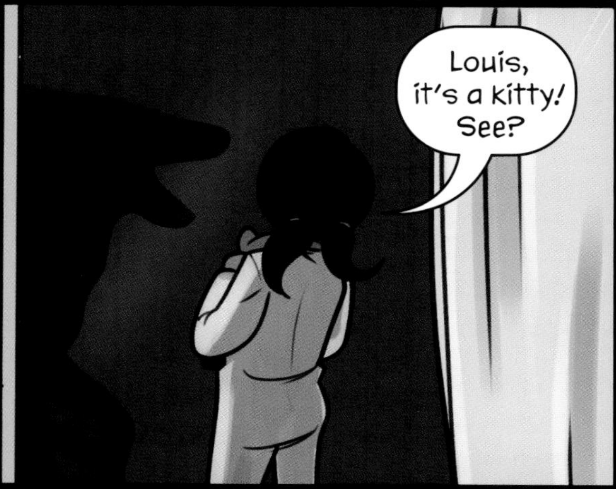
Louis, it's a kitty! See?

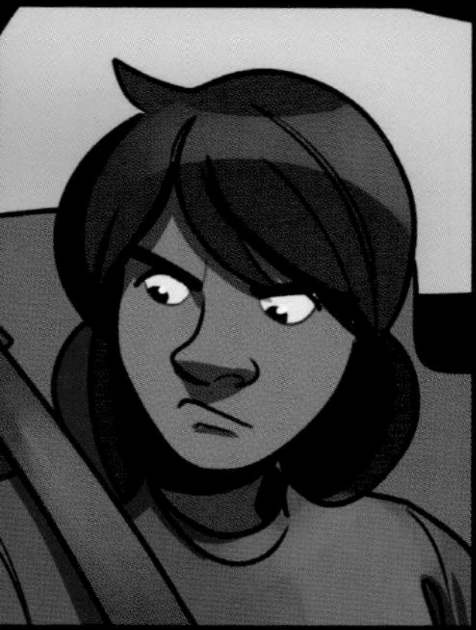

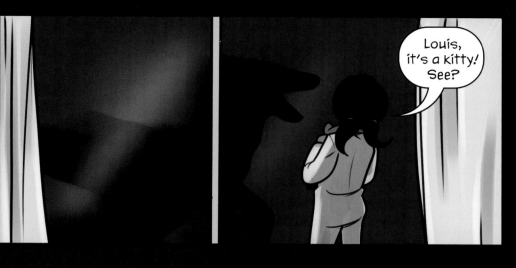

4. How has Louis changed from the start to the end of the story? Use examples to back up your answer.

5. What do you think will happen to the next kids who visit Prehistoric Action Park? Will they escape, or will they meet a different fate? Write the next chapter.

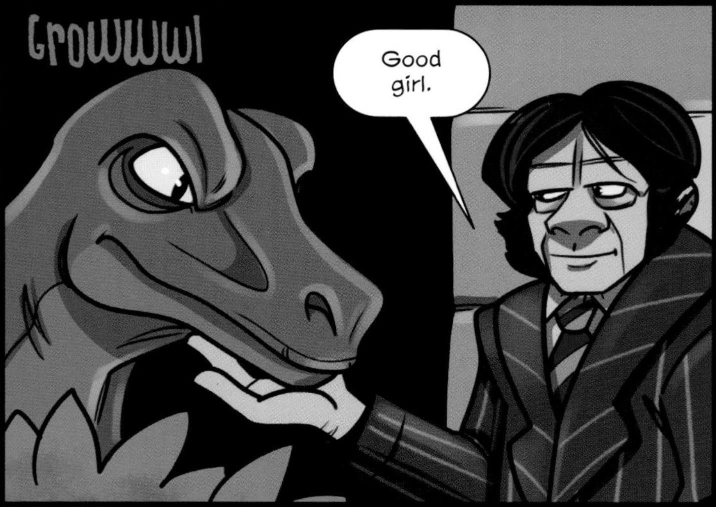
Growwwl
Good girl.

THE AUTHOR

Steve Foxe is the author of more than fifty children's books and comics properties including Spider-Ham, Batman, Pokémon, Transformers, Adventure Time, and Steven Universe, as well as other titles in Capstone's Scary Graphics and Far Out Fables series. He has also written a number of scary stories for adults . . . which you can read when you're older. He lives in Queens, New York, and has nothing but respect for modern-day dinosaurs: NYC street pigeons.

THE ILLUSTRATOR

Alan Brown is a freelance artist from the United Kingdom. He's worked on a variety of projects including Ben 10 Omniverse graphic novels for Viz Media, as well as children's book illustrations for the likes of HarperCollins and Watts. He has a keen interest in the comic book world, where he's at home creating bold graphic pieces. Alan works from an attic studio, along with his trusty sidekick, Ollie the miniature schnauzer, and his two sons, Wilf and Teddy.

GLOSSARY

attraction (uh-TRAK-shun)—an interesting thing for people to visit, see, or do

cruel (KROO-uhl)—causing great pain or hurt

extinct (ik-STINGKT)—died out and no longer living

insist (in-SIST)—to carry on with something in a strong, firm way

insult (in-SULT)—to say something rude or hurtful to someone

motel (moh-TEL)—a place by the road where people can stay and where the rooms are reached directly from an outdoor parking area

prehistoric (pree-hih-STOR-ik)—very old and from a time before history was recorded

sightseeing (SITE-see-ing)—related to the activity of visiting famous or interesting places

souvenir (soo-vuh-NEER)—something that is a reminder of a special place, event, or person

tourist trap (TOOR-ist TRAP)—a place that brings in many visitors and charges higher than normal prices

unbearable (uhn-BAIR-uh-buhl)—so bad or extreme that you can't put up with it

vacation (vay-KAY-shuhn)—a trip away from home to relax and have fun

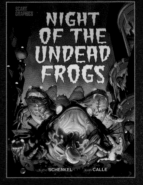